To Dad, with

xxx

THE COAST

Nigel Barley

VIKING

VIKING
Published by the Penguin Group
27 Wrights Lane, London W8 5TZ, England
Viking Penguin Inc., 40 West 23rd Street, New York, New York 10010, USA
Penguin Books Australia Ltd, Ringwood, Victoria, Australia
Penguin Books Canada Ltd, 2801 John Street, Markham, Ontario, Canada L3R 1B4
Penguin Books (NZ) Ltd, 182–190 Wairau Road, Auckland 10, New Zealand

Penguin Books Ltd, Registered Offices: Harmondsworth, Middlesex, England

First published 1990
1 3 5 7 9 10 8 6 4 2

Filmset in Monophoto Ehrhardt
Printed in Great Britain by Richard Clay Ltd, Bungay, Suffolk

A CIP catalogue record for this book is available from the British Library
ISBN 0–670–82829–7

PREFACE

This is a work of fiction. Its failures are failures of fiction, not of anthropology or history, and its truth is the truth of fiction and not that of any other universe of discourse. It deliberately brings together things that were not found at any single place or moment in West Africa in the nineteenth century, although virtually nothing has been simply invented. Thus the first mail contract, the existence of the Niger Coast Protectorate Force, the advent of tinned goods – all these may not have been noted in any single, eventful year. Similarly, I have not sought to clarify the differences between various masking societies in the coastal area – Ekpe, Ekpo, Egbo, etc. Nineteenth-century Europeans confused them and that confusion is a meaningful part of their view of Africa, that beneath a thin veneer all of it was in some sense 'the same'. They belong rather to that rich background against which events occur. As the Reverend Truscot would have observed, 'Every picture needs its light and shade.'

It will be obvious to anyone who has read up on West African history that I have drawn heavily on the Reverend Hope Waddell's *Twenty-nine Years in the West Indies and Central Africa*. Truscot himself owes much to that angular and irascible individual. Several incidents are drawn from his journal and it has occasionally proved impossible to improve on his own granitic humour or deadly accuracy of expression. Yet Truscot is not Waddell, and Akwa is not Calabar. Similarly, the pidgin English used here evokes rather than depicts the language still used on the Coast today. True pidgin would be incomprehensible to the speaker of standard English.

Yet the world depicted here is a real world. It corresponds to one encountered in the literature of the period and, indeed, is still largely intact in the coastal polities of southern Nigeria. There the visitor may still attend rites to worship gods and water spirits whose favourite food is bully beef and ship's biscuit and who tipple gin and sweet milky tea offered by a man in a Sherlock Holmes cape. It is the mark of that area to have taken elements from many cultures and brewed them into a thick, aromatic stew that is as distinctive and regional as a Lancashire hot-pot.

Nigel Barley

BOOK ONE

The very ground seemed to exhale moisture. It rolled in thick, billowy clouds of steam among the mangrove roots and dripped dankly from the leaves above. It trickled down the shells of the blue hairy crabs that stood watching, brandishing their claws in the red mud and blowing defiant froth. It streamed from the boots of the humans that they scuttled between when they finally abandoned bravado and fled. It splashed down on the mudskippers as they skidded over the reeking ooze blinking multilidded eyes. This was the end of a continent, a place of no firm divisions, where land and sea merged softly into each other and everything that lived either crept or slithered. Here any time of the day resembled a grey dusk or dawn, time without clear demarcations. The sky threw a chilly spatter of raindrops, fat and heavy, into the streams that swirled around the tiny island. They rattled against the cheap wood of the box, only slightly muted by the damp folds of the Union Jack.

Four pallbearers were more than enough to carry the last remains of Reverend Truscot, wasted as he was by fever to the mere manic idea of a fellow mortal. Yet the burden of his responsibility as man of God seemed to require a certain ponderousness. They teetered and slithered in the mud, wiping sweat and rain from brows and necks in watery despair. The rain drummed against black hats, new from England but already turning green with mould, and washed back from the lid of the box over their hands and down their sleeves.

Two Africans in flat caps and stripped to the waist leaned grinning on their shovels, one bare foot raised in anticipation of further spadework. Oblivious to the wetness coursing over their magnificent torsos, they watched the white men approach. Their splayed, bare toes dug deep into the mud around the hole. The blue scars running from their foreheads to the tips of their noses stood out stark beneath the varnish of moisture. When the party of white men got within ten feet of the grave, they bent down and began to bail out the turbid water with a calabash, looking for all the world like fisherwomen emptying a fish-trap. As fast as it was emptied out, the water flowed back in. It was no use, the water table here was just too high. They spat, broke off with shrugs and stepped back, their feet making sticky, sucking noises in the churned mire.

The white men, gasping and perspiring, tipped the box gratefully into the waiting puddle, sending a tidal wave over their boots. One whipped off the flag with the air of a conjuror who had made something disappear. But the deal box refused to disappear and floated defiantly on the surface. 'Contents, twelve Daneguns', they read on the lid, 'Made in Birmingham'. The last part at least was true. Reverend Truscot had been conceived in the upstairs room over his father's grocer's shop in that very town amidst the smell of camphor and cocoa. It was perhaps the search for the origin of these exotic odours of his conception that had led his questing feet over two continents.

One end of the box had been knocked out – the Reverend

being an unusually tall man – so that his head could poke through. The alternative would have been to break his legs, but that might have excited comment from the widow on the grounds of the unexpected abbreviation of her spouse. Out of deference for the sensibilities of the living, an old black silk hat had been rammed down over the staring eyes and nailed down to the wood, a common expedient in the Delta, where during the fever months gun-boxes were in even greater demand than their contents.

One of the black men leapt on to the coffin and bore down with his weight in a parody of dance steps as the other hastily shovelled thick clods of dirt on top. A choked gasp broke from the dark, dumpy form of the widow, anonymous under her weeds. A handkerchief fluttered in the shadows of the veil.

'A thing like this brings out the best in people. Jolly decent of Hauptmann's company to supply the box. Burial at sea, really ... If the box isn't properly under, they'll steal the pennies from his eyelids or cut off the head for ju-ju. You'd think *he*'d have come,' said Jones, stepping back from the edge and raising an umbrella. He fumbled in a back pocket and produced a hip-flask, took a shaky tug on it and passed it to the others. They all had the pale, papery skin that spoke of heat and fever, skin that lived in a tropical climate yet was never exposed to the sun. Around the eyes they had the bruised, heavy swags of flesh that came to men who had their first drink at ten in the morning and the odd sustaining snort at regular points thereafter. They were seldom exactly drunk and never exactly sober from the moment they rose swearing in the morning to the moment they tumbled befuddled into stained sheets at night. But all the time they wished they were some-where else – anywhere but here in this waste of creeks and swamps of the Niger Delta.

'He'll be here,' said Crosby, a sallow, prematurely aged man with a Liverpool whine. He wiped his glasses for the twentieth time that morning. 'He'll come if he can. As Head of the River, he's a stickler for that sort of thing – death of a white man and all that.' The flag hung dark and crushed in his hand like a drowned dog.

'He'll come if he's not laid up,' said a third. 'Last time I saw him he'd not been bit for a week and when the mosquitoes leave you alone, it's a sure sign the fever's coming.'

Shouts and curses eddied through the mist. Four more Krooboys, distinguished by the same facial scars as the grave-diggers, staggered in bearing a hammock of primitive construction, canvas slung between poles. Propped on cushions, haggard and bleached, was an elderly man leaning out and waving his cane. His face broke into an attempted smile more like the snarl of an old lion with its curved yellow teeth.

'Hallo, Jones, Miller, Crosby . . . Not dead yet you see. Put me down, you stupid buggers.'

The bearers set down the rickety structure and he clambered out with some difficulty. Adjusting straw hat and cane, straightening the stained jacket of his white cotton suit, he bowed cursorily towards the widow and toddled stiff-kneed towards the grave. He inclined his head towards Jones. 'Is he already in there?' he asked in a stage whisper. Jones nodded, thin-lipped as an undertaker, and held out the flask. With a guilty glance at the standing figures, he took a quick tug, passed it back and pulled a dog-eared prayer-book from his pocket.

The drone of his voice picked up to a steady pace. The watchers were a mixed bunch, worn-out white faces and impassive black ones, all men except for the widow. The Africans were, for the most part, shorter but hugely built – massive shoulders and legs – the legacy of a life of paddling canoes around the waterways. It was as if heat and moisture promoted animal as well as vegetal growth. They wore top hats, marks of their rank as chiefs, standing in poses of studied nonchalance with their hands splayed over the silver knobs of canes. Several flaunted cast-off cavalry topcoats, loud with gold braid and epaulettes, over the top of a skirt of chequered Madras print. They fussed with swords, fans and handkerchiefs like ladies at a dance. One wore an inverness cape encrusted with superfluous brass buttons, but cut of light check stuff that clung damply to his shoulders. Behind him stood a servant wearing a waistcoat over his bare chest and carrying a large silver snuff-box.

He leaned forward to bring his lips to the widow's ear. 'I sorry for Reverend,' he muttered in a whisky voice. 'He be good man too much. For sure, he go for God's castle.'

A paroxysm of sobs shook the dumpy, black frame that looked rather like a covered birdcage. Scarcely able to speak, she clutched wetly at his sleeve. 'Thank you ... King Jack. You know that he always respected ...' The King backed away, fluttering pink-tipped fingers in deprecation. His large brass ring caught the light.

From the graveside, Crosby watched. Smouldering, almond-shaped eyes swivelled to look at him, and Ali – the Reverend's Malay servant – stared him straight in the face, a smile passing lightly over his lips. There was something hard-edged and tight about that smile. 'He knows,' thought Crosby and a gush of fearful perspiration soaked him. 'He bloody knows.'

The words required by custom had been spoken at the graveside and the Head of the River turned and addressed the small crowd, less at ease now he had left the safety of a standard text and heckled by the irregular thump of the Krooboys driving a rough wooden cross into the mud.

'Funerals are not a time for long speeches. Anyway, I'm afraid I'm feeling pretty done up. Reverend Truscot is only the latest to fall prey to this fiendish climate. I'm glad at least he had the semblance of a decent burial. I suggest we all get under cover. There will be a reception – no, sorry, that's not the right word. There will be hospitality for those who want it on my hulk. As Head of the European traders, that's the least I can do. Not', he stammered quickly, 'that I want to do the least I can do . . . That is to say . . .' He abandoned all attempts at lucidity with a weary wave of the hand, climbed aboard the hammock and began to shout and rave at the Krooboys, who grinned good-naturedly and hitched him up like an ill-fitting pair of trousers. This creole of contempt, a koine of oaths, pidgin names for body parts and synonyms of violent death, was the only language conventionally used on the Coast to communicate from white to black. Only strangers noticed it or took exception to it. Its existence was often invoked as one of the reasons no white woman could ever live in this place and it was wielded as a blunt weapon against those few who ever tried.

The procession set off in the disorderly trudge of people who have trodden the same route too often before, minds plunged into the swamp of present physical discomfort. This was the 'bad bush', where had to be flung those bodies that were an offence to the earth. That Truscot had been permitted interment at all was a considerable concession on the part of the King of Akwa, disqualified as he had been by swollen feet and diarrhoea, both indubitable signs of witchcraft – but then white men worked differently from black and everyone knew they could not be witches. The Akwans were all perfectly well aware of the real reason the white men were so insistent on hiding their dead – they cut off their heads for ju-ju.

This mutual distrust in the matter of heads went back to a brutish, early expedition mounted by the Germans. One of their party dying, they had carried his head back to Germany, seeing this as the only way of preventing mutilation of his corpse by the fierce head-hunters they knew to inhabit these parts. After their departure, the Akwans, curious to learn more about white men, did indeed disinter the body, but were appalled to see that white men were such benighted savages as to behead their own people – something no Akwan could ever do.

There was a sudden sound of wet tearing, as of a great sail splitting in a gale. It spun them round. The widow emitted a muffled wail, choking back a scream through a wet wodge of handkerchief. The white men gasped and gawped. The Kroo-boys, pop-eyed, dropped the handles of the hammock, so that the Head of the River lay sprawled in the mud. The King clutched the amulet pendant around his neck and raised his stick in a futile gesture of threat.

The coffin had risen up like a *croûton* from the soup of mud into which it had been plunged. The rain began to wash the dirt off the gleaming top hat that bobbed jauntily up and down, nodding a knowing greeting from the dead. Only Ali smiled that light and pure smile. He was quite unmoved by the Reverend's anticipation of the Last Trump, a theological anomaly they had often debated. It did not matter. After all, there was nothing in the box but rocks. He should have put in more rocks.

Reverend Truscot's Journal

Our eighth week at sea in constant bad weather – preserved only by the Lord's hand. We long for dry land and dry clothes; despite our perpetual endeavour we can attain, it seems, neither. Relations with the Captain have been strained and devoid of warmth. After putting out from the Canaries, it seemed to me that the head of the boat was a little down and I brought this to the Captain's attention. The Captain brusquely denied it and suggested I should tend to my own trade and leave the running of the ship to those who knew best. Two days later, when trying to find rest in my cabin, I clearly heard water washing back and forth behind the wall. A sustained altercation with the Captain was necessary before the bilges were pumped and yielded gallons of water. Inspection revealed an uncaulked seam down low near the water-line. Repair had not been difficult but unheeded might well have cost us the ship. I sought, as ever, to be generous to the frailty of others and in my sermon that Sunday I preached to the ship's company concerning the foolish virgins with their untrimmed wicks, seeking to show that negligence had Biblical precedent, that carelessness was a more constant danger than studied evil. But the Captain, in his pride, took it ill. His wick, he felt, was not untrimmed, and he fell out of fellowship with us. For this reason, I could offer him no comfort in the perilous passage into the river, though I might easily have made valuable suggestions.

The Reverend Emmanuel Truscot had arrived in a dampness as all-pervasive as that of his departure. Had he been capable of speech he would doubtless have pointed to that circularity as an edifying model of the vanity of human endeavour without divine grace. He was wont to perceive divine patterns in the everyday dross of the experiential world. He stood at the bow of the little *Ethiope* staring off towards where he imagined the banks of the river to be, seeing nothing but serried ranks of mist. Yet his optimism created a clear vision in his mind of the rosy prospects that awaited them. After all, the King himself had requested a missionary. They could not but succeed.

The other passengers were still huddled below, rolling their eyes and – doubtless – whimpering. Only a gaggle of young Krooboys from Sierra Leone, deck passengers who were forbidden to go downstairs, hung on to the rigging and laughed. With the arrogance of their young strength they sprawled carelessly across the deck. Without their steady, reliable labour European penetration of the Coast would be impossible, but there was something Europeans found galling in their self-assurance, the lightness with which they touched the earth. They would be on the way to hire themselves out for a year as labourers and should be anxious. One, he knew, would have been on the Coast before and be acting as foreman, negotiating their wages and taking one month out of the twelve for his commission. At the end of their engagement, they would hop on another vessel back to their country with a box full of trinkets that would either be lost in the surf of Las Palmas or stripped from them by relatives. Only the lucky ones would hang on to enough to buy a wife. They laughed again. Truscot smiled, loving them for their cheerful innocence.

The *Ethiope* had just crossed the sandbar at the mouth of the River Akwa, where thundering rollers had crushed many a ship, so that wood and rusted anchors littered the coast thereabouts, like starfish and seaweed a normal shore. The Captain, a cool and distressingly godless man, had stood steadfast on the bridge, as if in emulation of the rocks beneath, impassively noting the soundings called out by a seaman at the prow and silently grasping the rails with his hands. They had waited half a day in vain for a pilot to appear before the Captain elected to risk the passage himself. Reverend Truscot had seen the white knuckles on those hands as the soundings ran swiftly down from ten fathoms to two and they had scraped bottom before the rasping voice of the sailor had called out, 'Five fathoms!' Then they knew they were over the bar and into clear water. He had prayed, not for himself but for Mary, his wife, and for God's work in this land of darkness. He had known that prayer would be heard. There were fine souls here to be won in the contest with the Devil.

An awkward, angular figure, he slithered and slipped to the rear of the bucking vessel. Mary stood at the taffrail with Ali, her eyes tight shut, too terrified to speak, gripping her handkerchief in her teeth. He looked at her dumpy, pasty figure and felt that love that has pity as its closest relation. When he offered comfort, she waved him wordlessly away. Ali was of a race of sure-footed sailors, almost amphibious, and turned towards him a face of seraphic calm and confidence that somehow unnerved him still further.

For their belief was not the same belief, their god not the same god. Ali was a Muslim of a sure and certain faith. Hard indeed had been the battle to be allowed to bring him here from their previous station in Singapore. But he knew that Mary would not be parted from him, as Ali would not lightly leave them. She had given up everything else, house, friends, the pleasant circle of a devout following, to come with him here. He could not rob her of faithful Ali as well. They had worked together with a closeness of fit that bore the stamp of inevitability – nay, divine will. That was the way it was. It could not easily be changed.

Good, totally honest Ali had cheered them up in the brooding atmosphere of the Captain's resentment. He had amazed the sailors with his tricks of Buginese sea-craft. A favourite was to whip the spare sarong off his head and sling it round the mast. Then, leaning back against the loop so formed, he could run lightly to the top of the highest rigging and slide, like a feather, down again. The phlegmatic old tars had stamped and clapped their sea-wise hands. Ali had the rare gift of making friends everywhere, a natural warmth that mellowed Truscot's own northern reserve.

The water, slower moving now, became a softer hue, like brown Windsor soup, as if yielding to their unspoken entreaties. The bucking changed to an insidious undulation that was yet more unpleasant. Then, as if a great engine had been turned off, they were of a sudden in calm water. The air stilled about them. A pestilential heat descended, blended with a reek of rotting vegetation that made poor Mary gag. Sweat began to course down their faces. The malarial miasma that breeds disease from the swamp closed over them.

A dug-out canoe appeared alongside, propelled by three lethargic men with pointed paddles carved with snakes and fish. Mary gasped. They were stark naked. '*Orang gagak*, "crow people",' said Ali with interest. In their midst, unsullied by effort, sat a portly figure as clothed as they were unclothed, as if he had assumed their unwanted dress like a cricket umpire. On his head he wore a knitted cap pulled over the crown of a felt hat. On his hands were gloves. Yet his manner of climbing the rope that trailed out behind the *Ethiope* was lively enough. '*Orang monyet*, "monkey people",' corrected Ali with satisfaction. Truscot had heard the term somewhere before. Where? Of course! It was what whites called the Malays.

The clothed figure had reached the bridge and executed a military salute. The Captain extended a hand, but not in greeting. He was asking for something. Puzzled, they watched as a brass badge was passed over. The Captain studied it and handed it back.

'Well, Mr Long John. Your credentials are in order. Better late than never. Take the helm and God help you if you run her aground.'

'They have African river pilots?' Mary asked.

'The rivers are African,' Truscot remarked gently, his blue eyes suddenly flashing. Mary bit her lip. As usual the reproof was so gentle as to seem almost a product of her own imagination.

The shore at last became visible, a soggy yet somehow blasted desert of black slime washed down by a thousand miles of river, pushed up in places into hillocks. At the water's edge mangrove trees perched on high roots and plunged aerial suckers into the filth like feeding spiders. To either side minor channels led off into the dark swamps, a maze of tangled muddy channels. It was here that the ships of the British West Africa Squadron played hide-and-seek with the slave vessels of Portugal and Spain as they sought to dodge the newly imposed embargo on the export of human cargo to the Americas. In the distance lay what must be the town of Akwa, a dispiriting heap of wooden shacks piled atop an elevated mudbank, a workmen's shanty town erected while waiting for some nobler structure to go up on the site. 'Each one founded on human misery and cemented with blood,' Truscot recalled the words of the Captain spoken in more friendly times. A fleet of tiny canoes, powered by naked pulla-boys, swarmed out like flies around the vessel, the Captain bellowing to them to keep clear. As the ship awkwardly manoeuvred, one was struck by the bow and thrust under the water, only to re-emerge with its laughing owner clinging to its bottom. He dived underneath the craft and rolled it back the right way up, bracing himself against the sides with his feet. Truscot found himself clapping and waving. Ali watched. He would add that trick to his repertoire.

There was a stirring from below. The other passengers, who had been cowering there, began to boil up over the decks with bundles of possessions tied in brightly coloured cloths. Fat mammies with toiling hams surged across the deck, claiming prominence and depositing burdens in ill-smelling profusion. Children squalled and puked. A bellow of muted rage rose from a hundred throats. Black men in European clothes with cardboard suitcases shouted and waved fists, dashing for the places nearest the side, summoning the pulla-boys and trampling the women in their eagerness to debark. The women fought back with mighty sweeps of their huge behinds and meaty forearms. Truscot thought unwillingly of Irish washerwomen in London. Somewhere (a music hall in his youth? No, a Belfast student in the seminary) he had heard the witticism,

'Irish women have received a dispensation from the Pope allowing them to wear their arms upside down so that they grow thicker towards the wrists.' So, it seemed, had Akwa ladies.

Dispute had gelled about various points of localized conflict. He had seen this phenomenon before when the ship had stopped in Sierra Leone. It was the standard African argument. There an African passenger had walked off with some luggage that apparently belonged to a fellow countryman. When apprehended, however, the fellow had conducted the ensuing discussion not in terms of the ownership of the baggage, but entirely at the most abstract level of the right of his interlocutors to question him or restrain him at all.

Similarly, Truscot knew that by now everyone would have lost sight of the original source of the dispute beneath him. Each side would be enumerating in pidgin, and at lavish length, the general principles of natural justice, if not international law, raised by the present situation. People glared and screamed at each other, waved fists but only delivered the slightest of body nudges. Truscot smiled to himself. He and Mary would have to wait aboard ship until the formalities with the King had been completed, so they were free to contemplate these colourful small fish. Truscot felt his heart going out to them. It was the disorder of life.

'Appalling!' gasped Mary, turning to Ali on the rear deck. 'Why don't they wait their turn?'

Ali shrugged. It was the sort of behaviour one would expect of the Chinese. Black men were like the Chinese. One should not expect too much of them. The riot continued. Possessions rained down upon the heads of the boatmen, people trod over each other in the wobbly canoes, risking immersion. Someone unwisely sought to raise an umbrella and was knocked sideways into the murky water. 'Plenty sharks in here I reckon,' volunteered Ali with a delicious shiver.

The onboard disputes gave way before intense haggling over the fare to be charged for conveyance to the dock. The boatmen folded their arms and sulked. Everyone screamed and raged for a few minutes more, then cheerfully they began rowing towards a wooden pier, pausing a judicious distance from it to collect payment in cowrie shells. Truscot smiled again. It recalled to him innocent childhood games on the beach, the treasures of boyhood – the bartering of stones, a cockle shell, once a piece of coral brought back by an uncle.

Truscot had dispatched Ali to the market in Lagos with a sovereign to convert into this small change and been amazed to see him return with ten women, each of whom bore a largish sack on her head. It seemed that 20,000 were to be had for twelve shillings and sixpence – minus, of course, the cost of their porterage, which amounted to almost a quarter of the load. They had been surprised that Truscot did not want to count them. Perhaps he had misunderstood, but by gesture they had seemed to suggest that they, too, might be procurable for a few cowries more. He had chased the thought away. One should not blame other people for what might be one's own failures to comprehend.

Ali had been delighted, looking round with shining eyes and clapping his hands together. '*Tuan*, we're rich!' Now Truscot wondered idly how much it would cost to get the money from the ship to the harbour, then from the harbour to their lodgings. Would anything be left at all?

Mary seems strangely unexcited by our arrival in this new field where we shall cultivate souls for the Lord. She is doubtless gathering strength for the struggle to come. But before we can reap, we must sow. Before we can sow, we must clear the land of weeds and other rank growth. But before we clear the land, we must gain title to it.

It was not until the next day that King Jack came aboard to 'break trade' – to fix prices for the ship's cargo and receive his 'dash' of copper bracelets, the larger money of the Coast. In his honour the ensign had been hoisted and seven guns fired off in the brassy face of the sun. The galley had been a madhouse of activity the whole morning, with all hands pressed into service as pantry boys and with boats plying between the ship and shore bearing supplies. Yams, dwarf cattle, eggs and fruits had been hauled aboard in a concentrated African cornucopia that gladdened Reverend Truscot's eye. An awning had been stretched over the deck to provide shade and seamen set to peeling, plucking and pulverizing in anticipation of King Jack's coming. Others sat around in innocent and godly pursuits such as carving palm-nut kernels into necklaces. 'For loved ones at home?' he had asked. They had laughed and exchanged stage winks. 'That's right, Reverend. For our wives.' Later, Ali's sharper eyes would see them around the necks of every harlot in Akwa, as now he alone detected the signs of their previous night's debauch on trade gin.

Reverend Truscot and his party hovered disconsolately on deck, feeling the impossibility of simultaneously keeping out of everyone's way at once. This morning, however, the Captain seemed unusually disposed to converse and beckoned them almost matily over to the side nearest the town. His face was unable to accommodate a smile, but it at least moderated its fixed scowl. He nodded towards the town with a bristly chin.

'The King will be coming aboard for "chop" – food – any time now. The old devil's a stickler for being shown due deference.'

'How will we know him?'

The Captain laughed bitterly, 'Oh, you'll know him all right. His sable majesty has a countenance compounded of guile, suspicion and mendacity in equal proportions. Apart from that, he'll be wearing a brass crown.'

19

A large canoe with twenty paddlers put out from the shore, a faded English ensign fluttering from the stern overlaid with the words 'King Jack' executed in crimson plush. A small brass cannon was fired off from the front in salute as the vessel slipped at irregular pace over the harbour. In the centre, on a chair of elaborately European manufacture, sat a tall figure with complexion of such darkness as to glow almost blue in the sunlight. Around him, at slightly lower levels, perched a collection of wild and raffish figures, whose accoutrement seemed to have been assembled from the barrows of used-clothing dealers. Some wore spats around bare ankles, others waistcoats of watered silk over bare chests. One sported a lopsided periwig somewhat down over one ear and, around his neck, a collection of bones and feathers that would have done credit to a gamekeeper's pantry. From time to time he held up a large brass bell and waggled it into the wind like a muffin seller. A swarm of flies followed him faithfully, rising humming from his shoulders whenever he rang the bell, only to settle again. Several of the men sported Daneguns – the long, smooth-barrelled rifles that could be loaded with any old iron fragments, stones or nails and fired off at approximately equal risk to owner and target. From time to time they discharged their pieces into the air, taking care to hold them at arm's length lest they explode in their owners' faces. This was the usual firing position. Akwa riflemen were not noted for their marksmanship. Their guns were the music of war rather than weapons of offence.

The canoe circled the ship twice and finally approached the end of a rope ladder that had been let down over the side. The man with the brass bell leant forward and very deliberately crushed a chicken's egg against the hull.

'The ju-ju chief,' explained the Captain. 'I've no doubt you'll disapprove, but without that egg, no trade if I stay here a twelvemonth. The natives won't come near the boat.'

'Why does he ring that bell, Captain?' asked Mary.

'That's Ekpo, another native fetish. It's an organization after the manner of the Masons. All the powerful men get together under the ju-ju. If anyone owes them money, they send out a masked runner and put Ekpo on his house. He can't leave it, on pain of death, till he pays. Even the slaves can enter the lower grades to get protection for their lives and property, but higher grades cost up to a thousand pound, so that's for the big traders.'

'You mean the African traders?'

A gleam of malice shone in his eye. 'That I do not. I mean what I say. Many of the white men here have joined. It's a fine way of sorting your debtors. It seems to me we could use it at home.'

Truscot felt a bristling irritation begin under his scalp and suffuse his whole body. Before he could make answer, however, the Captain turned away to greet the King, who was at that moment hauling his frame over the side, fussily pulling a metal ladies' tiara from his bosom and thrusting it on his head as one would push a custard pie in a man's face. Yet there was a sort of unexpected dignity about his features that somehow over-whelmed the comic effect of the bauble. Someone thrust a cane into his hand and he struck a posture as if 'making a leg'. The Captain executed a stiff, reluctant little bow emulated by Truscot and Ali. Mary picked at her disordered mousy hair and swept the ground with a low curtsy. The King's face split into a broad grin, revealing large square teeth like serried gravestones. His attendants crowded gawping behind him, shyly, like boys at a fair. Truscot noted that they had left their guns in the sloop. The chair was now passed over the side together with a collection of barbarously carved stools. Everyone sat down. A large umbrella was most inconveniently erected over the King, but, because of the low canvas awning, forced down so as to

21

obscure most of his face, making conversation a very peek-a-boo affair.

'What fashion people be this?' King Jack waved his cane at Truscot's group.

The Captain smirked. 'This be Liverpool ju-ju king, with wife and slave.'

Truscot opened his mouth to protest, then thought better of it. There would be time to refine such rough-hewn equivalences later. Ali muttered to himself.

'You first white woman ever I see,' commented the King with interest. Mary flushed under his frank top-to-toe perusal. 'How many pickanin' you got? How much you cost? How many other wife? Why you not fat?'

Mary stammered, 'I . . . well . . . that is . . .'

The King pouted and swivelled his gaze round to Ali. 'You not white slave. You like when white man go with Akwa woman. Pickanin' brown like you. We got plenty here too much like that. We call them "Mammy Wata boy". Your Captain got plenty here like that. Maybe he your fadder too?'

Truscot felt Ali stiffen. The Captain seemed to be gripped by a coughing fit. Enough of diplomatic niceties. Truscot stepped forward. It was time to engage Africa.

'King,' he interposed swiftly in the voice he used for sermons, 'some time ago you signed a treaty with Lieutenant Needham of HMS *Rattler* when you abandoned the slave trade. He was sent by the great white queen. You said you wanted a missionary in your country at that time to advise you on God's law. We have come to answer your call.' He handed him a large leather-bound volume. 'I bring you God's holy word that you may know eternal life and never die.'

The King grinned expansively and slapped his thigh with the Bible. 'With this book I never die? You think I fool black man for sure. Even my ju-ju king,' he indicated the fetish-clad figure by his side, 'no knock off death one time. Bonny get mission. Calabar get mission. People there still die. For why I no get this thing? You teach my people sabby book. That good for trade. White men chop us till we like to die because we no sabby book. It be fool fashion. You give me shakehands. You live for Akwa.'

Reverend Truscot stepped forward and proffered his hand in manly greeting. The King stared at it with distaste.

'Don't be a damn fool, Reverend,' muttered the Captain in a stage whisper. 'He doesn't want your hand. "Shakehands" is money you have to pay to set up shop here.'

Truscot felt the heat of anger begin to rise in his gorge again. 'You want money from me to bring the word of God to you? King, understand this well. I am no trader. I make no profit in gold – I mean copper. If a man give you his daughter, would you want money from him too? If a man give you the dinner from his table, would you want him to pay you to eat it? If a man give you the greatest gift of divine truth, would you want him to pay for that?' His rage fed on itself, growing as he spoke. His stick-like figure shook with it. The hawkish nose hacked at the air.

King Jack looked taken aback by such vehemence. Then he laughed again. 'This be no sweet mouth palaver. You strong too much. I no like God-palaver. Liverpool man put your God-palaver for that paper. I no ask for missionary but he make me set my hand to that paper. I no got time for you now. You go come my house tomorrow. It no be fit we talk now. This time for trade palaver.'

The various goods were brought up and ranged in heaps before the monarch and his retinue, cheap Manchester cloths, brassware, mirrors, Daneguns, squareface gin – cheap potato spirit from Hamburg at tuppence halfpenny a quart – gun-powder. One by one they were handled and a price fixed in coppers. Truscot noted with displeasure that this price was about three times what he might have considered reasonable, based on the experience of his father's shop. The King and his henchmen reserved a number of items for their personal dash. Haggling was extended and exhausting, and the Reverend Truscot, being stolidly ignored, took himself off to the after-deck to ponder on this sad reception.

'Take heart, Mannie,' Mary consoled. She looked at him with perfect trust in her currant-bun face and squeezed his hand. 'We are not here alone. The Lord is with us.'

Her words were drowned by the firing of a gun to announce that trade was opened.

In another part of the ship Ali was deep in conclave with an immaculate young Negro in Western dress, King Jack's son, Prince John Bull. They were sharing a dish of pungent spiced beef prepared by Ali, rolling mashed yam into little balls, pressing a concavity into them and using them to scoop up hot sauce.

'You cook well, my friend. I think we will be brothers. We must eat quick. If my father finds me eating food not tested for poison, he'll kill me.'

They laughed and shook hands loosely, then clicked their middle fingers together after the manner of the Coast. Somewhere on the way Ali had mastered the art.

'You speak English very well.'

'English? Oh, you mean Liverpool. England is part of Liverpool. Yes, I speak Liverpool. I worked for one of the Liverpool traders here since I was a small boy. My father, King Jack, apprenticed me in trade to Mr Crosby. He said we must learn their ways.' A frown passed over his pleasant, open face. 'They are strange people, though.'

Ali laughed. 'Very strange.'

'When I was a boy, the Liverpool king, Brother George, sent his men here to say we must sell him slaves and not sell them to other nations. They made us promise slaves and if we could not find them they said we were bad, turned their guns on our town and set fire to it. Then they came and said they would not buy our slaves any more and when we sold them to other Liverpool ships, again they said we were bad and turned their guns on our town. So we sold our slaves to other nations and again the Liverpool men came and said we had done wrong and fined us in our own country. Every year they changed their mind on what is good and what bad. How do they live in that place? I would go crazy, for sure.

'Now they try to make us knock off killing our own slaves because it is against white men's fashion. But, of course, we still do. It is right that when big man dies he does not go to the spirit world as a pauper. They tell us not to drink and sell us gin, and not to fight and sell us guns. And they are always drunk and firing guns themselves. It is very strange.

'My father does not want missionaries here telling him, "You do this. You knock off that." He says they spy for the Liverpool men how to take the country. But when the navy men come with their big guns, all you must do is make crosses on their papers and then they are happy and go away again. It seems to me white men are very stupid.'

'When your father dies, will you be king here?'

'Maybe. It depends on the big men.' He sprawled his massive limbs across the deck in demonstration. 'I am still small boy. It depends when my father dies. I am too young now. Maybe my uncle Duke Bosun will kill me and take the throne. Maybe I'll kill him first.' He finished eating and put down the dish, rinsed his hands in a basin and carefully dried them on his socks.

'But . . .' Ali hesitated, 'can he do that if the Liverpool men are against it?'

'No, that's for sure. The Consul has the power to break the king. If the river gentlemen here oppose him, he can send the warship to spoil the town or close the river and stop trade. He did it before in the time of King Robert when a trader's house was burnt down and his clerk eaten. No man here can be king unless Consul agree.'

'So ... It would be a good thing for you if there were a missionary here who liked you and saw you as a friend of white men's fashion, someone who could help you with the Consul. Then Duke Bosun could not harm you.'

A cloud lifted from the Prince's face. 'That's true. But in Akwa there are many ways to kill a man.' He looked down at his food doubtfully. 'Maybe I should talk to my father about it. It is not always good to be too much with one side or the other. As Liverpool men say, "You must keep a foot in both pies."'

Good news this morning! The King has sent his son, a most civil youth who promises well, to announce his change of heart. It seems we are to receive land and permission to work among the people here. Truly, the Lord works in a mysterious way to soften a heathen's feelings in the silent watches of the night! An interesting fact is that this youth's English is almost without accent, which refutes the common belief that Negroes are unable to properly pronounce our tongue because of the form of their lips. Yet I cannot subscribe to the other folly that an African brought up in England would speak the tongue exactly after the fashion of an Englishman. Can a cow bark?

The first resident of the town encountered by Reverend Truscot on disembarkation was a very large iguana lizard. As he assisted Mary from the canoe, the brute – some four feet long – waddled up and, after a few peremptory flicks of its tongue, fell to ecstatically licking the blacking from Truscot's boots. Truscot, a lover of almost all God's creatures, had been delighted.

'Look, Mary. What a pretty thing! It must like the pig-fat in the blacking.' Mary, perceiving that it would soon have exhausted the Reverend's footwear and might well move on to her own, held down her skirts and urged him to hurry on. He stroked its head gently with his toe, drawing a groan of amazement from the loiterers on the pier. It rubbed itself against him like a cat. In a way this was a most fortunate predilection on the part of the reptile. The iguana was held in awe by the local populace; indeed, they would suffer none to kill it nor even harm it, deeming it to be the messenger of the chief deity, himself – or, as some said, herself – a somewhat shadowy figure best approached through the lizard. When questioned by Truscot on the subject of their local god, a resident would have defined it according to a simple theology. 'God made all things. Our duty is to throw him crumbs when we chop and gin when we drink. We ask from him one thing – to kill those first who want to kill us.'

The bystanders who witnessed the encounter between Truscot and the lizard rushed to spread the news, so that before he had left the harbour, he was thronged by vast crowds convinced that the deity had shown its personal approval of the mission.

'Isn't it surprising that even the savage's heart may be moved by a little kindness shown to animals?' mused Truscot. 'Who would have thought it? That the tiger should show mercy to the bleating lamb.'

Mary crushed her handkerchief to her face against the sweet stench of excrement that dotted the beach, turds dissolving slowly in the lapping waves. The crowds smiled and laughed, reaching out to touch them. The women stroked Mary's hair and clutched her hands to their bosoms with shrieks of delight, held out their babies or their bellies swollen by pregnancy. Lepers, those afflicted by running sores and seething pocks, rubbed their ailing parts against the couple in innocent hope of improvement. Their clothes became spotted with the palm-oil with which the ladies anointed their skins. In the narrow streets the press of even good-natured, unwashed humanit — largely in the dress of Eden — became oppressive. Mary felt herself suffocating. The hands in her face were like the wings of birds, the fingers like spiders. She sobbed and broke away, Truscot chasing after her as after a disobedient dog. They fled, they knew not whither, between the houses, the howling and screaming dinning in their ears.

Buildings had been erected without thought of town-planning, in a higgledy-piggledy fashion. The land had not been levelled first and they were constantly obliged to climb and descend into pools of ordure or heaps of discarded rubbish trapped between two higher sections. Sleek rats and ponderous iguanas watched them agate-eyed. Chickens scattered at their passage. The greater part of the town seemed to have been built on discarded periwinkle shells. Everywhere people were chewing absently on the molluscs and spitting out the shells, so that the older buildings seemed to be sinking into the ground. Everywhere wandered scabby, neglected-looking sheep, their wool caked to their bodies with mud and reeking excrement. Truscot pursed his lips. When it came to the stage of Bible translation, there would be problems here. He could not compare the relation between priest and Man to that between a shepherd — for they had none — and these despised and degraded creatures. For the time being best stick to 'fishers of men'. They would understand that all right.

The dwellings themselves were mostly miserable hovels of wattle-and-daub construction, eked out occasionally with rusty corrugated iron. They leaned and sagged against each other. Often, unusual materials had been incorporated with great ingenuity. One had walls of empty squareface gin bottles, combining the owner's addiction with utility, another a roof of brass pans hammered flat, a third sported portholes looted from a wreck. What were clearly the dwellings of important men, square structures of rough red brick with cement trim, were marked out with cannon or huge iron cauldrons for boiling palm-oil. At the threshold of each, the skull of a vanquished enemy was set into the ground, and all entering or leaving contrived to step upon it.

They dodged and ducked under the low eaves in the maze of houses, wandering deeper and deeper, with the crowd howling on their heels, pushing them from behind like hounds after the fox. Mary covered her ears and began to wail softly. The paths were too narrow to permit Truscot to put his arm around her, so he seized her hand behind him and led her as elephants are said to wander trunk to tail.

Suddenly, a gate opened before them and a smiling figure extended his hand in courtly greeting. He was of a height with Truscot. Could it be Prince John Bull? Truscot looked help-lessly into the pleasant, friendly face and suddenly realized that all Akwa people looked the same to him, like eighteenth-century portraits in a gallery – all you saw was periwigs and sharp noses. He could not be sure of this man's identity. Whoever it was, he was friendly and was beckoning them in, a very present help in trouble.

'Oh, quick, quick, Mannie,' Mary gasped, galled by his slowness, and pushed anxiously clenched fists into his back. Gratefully, they slid through the aperture and the gate was bolted behind them.

Inside was a large open space of clean sand, swept and raked, pleasantly soft to the feet. Such was the profligacy of vegetal growth on the Coast that local notions of gardening consisted entirely of deracination and extirpation. In the centre rose a structure that pulled them up short. Mary ceased to wail, stared open-mouthed and started to giggle.

The house had been imported wholesale from Liverpool and set on a foundation of mangrove poles. It was based on a standard suburban villa of the expanding English cities, but instead of bricks and mortar, it was of galvanized iron sections bolted together over a wooden frame. A balustrade, complete with cast-iron lions, encased the stairway that led up to the raised ground floor. Each storey of the three-tier structure was surrounded by a veranda with a different animal theme. On the ground floor each support was surmounted by a unicorn – interpreted locally as an emaciated rhinoceros. The first floor boasted sporting dolphins, rearing up like begging dogs. The top floor displayed eagles hunched in saturnine splendour and picked out in gold paint. The *pièce de résistance*, however, was the gargoyles, each in the image of Queen Victoria, complete with crown, painted in vivid colour and with pouting lips ready to spew forth rain collected from the entire expanse of the roof. Underneath, deep holes had been eroded in the sand by the flow of water. A large British ensign hung limp on the galvanized roof, one corner snagged on a weather-vane in the form of a storm-tossed galleon. Above the door was bolted a cast-iron sign, 'King Jack's Castle'. Heraldic angels, picked out in gold paint, trumpeted forth the glory of the name.

The Prince, for he it surely must be, led them up the staircase and clapped his hands politely at the entrance. Since there was no response from within, he bowed them into the waiting room and begged them to sit while they waited. He himself would seek out his father in his private quarters above.

The Reverend Truscot and his wife peered inside and insinuated themselves with difficulty through the doorway. At first they thought they had been shown in error to some store-room for unwanted furniture. A vast profusion of the most indescribable bric-à-brac was spread before them. *Chaise-longues*, sofas and chairs were so pressed together that it was impossible to gain access to any without climbing over them.

Moreover, no consensus had been reached concerning which way they should face, so that the impression, which may well have corresponded to the truth, was that the royal household consisted exclusively of warring factions determined to turn their backs on each other. Betwixt and between them had been jammed a mass of small tables, sideboards, hat-stands and whatnots, each groaning beneath an accumulated weight of heavy blue glassware, Delft pottery, china animals and children's dolls. Ironically, the legs of each item of furniture were chastely shrouded with frills, whereas the lower limbs of humanity were everywhere flaunted naked in Akwa. Clocks seemed to be especially dear to the King's heart, for twenty or thirty of the most ornate and hideous variety were distributed over the room. Although every single one was busily ticking and whirring, all told a different hour. A neat simile, thought Truscot, for a sermon on the different sects of the Christian faith.

The walls were covered from a height of about three feet up to the ceiling with mirrors, paintings of Highland scenes and stuffed exotic beasts. The Reverend Truscot removed a beaver with bared fangs from a sofa and climbed into it. Mary struggled in behind and began to repair her appearance in one of the liver-spotted mirrors, wiping perspiration and smudges from her forehead. The fabric of the chairs smelled of damp and decay, while the iron walls radiated a fierce heat, trapped and concentrated by thick, plush curtains.

Seasonal damp had encouraged mould to sprout from every surface in thick green fur and curled veneer. Dry heat had split the wood and drained molten glue from the joints so that they were sprung and gaped emptily, like the mouths in Truscot's first Glasgow parish. Termites worked furiously, mining the wood beneath the surface, leaving only a paper-thin simulacrum of furniture to deceive the eye. Over all lay the thick red dust blown on the dry harmattan wind from the Sahara desert.

'Mannie,' Mary whispered, 'how do you suppose the person who brought all this in ever got out again?' They laughed together. It was a good sound. She looked at him adoringly. Theirs had been an odd match. She had never been a particularly godly woman, but assumed godliness as wives shrug on the tastes of those they wed. She had taken to religion as she had given up sweet puddings, which Truscot abominated. She had never once told him how much she hated Singapore, the savagery, the heat, the flying cockroaches. Her lack of complaint had been taken for quiet satisfaction. She knew that he loved her, but it was not an *active* sort of love. There had never been poetry and sighs, just respectful affection and a proposal of marriage phrased in terms of mutual suitability and the demands of good sense. Mannie's trouble was that he loved the whole world. It was not possible to be jealous of the whole world. She shook off such thoughts, stood up and looked out into the yard. 'Oh my!'

From their vantage point they could see into the outhouses that crowded up to the rear of the building, like the begging poor about a great house. They were little more than roofs resting on stout mangrove poles with double doors forming the two long sides. On one side they opened on to the yard, on the other on to a beach of alluvial mud. Squads of men, stripped to a scanty loincloth, laboured in the damp heat unloading goods from the *Ethiope* via small canoes. Barrels of powder were being rolled towards a stone-built shed, the old barracoons formerly used as temporary cages for slave cargoes. Crates of squareface were stacked everywhere, shining glassy green in the sun. Further along the beach, puncheons of palm-oil to make soap for white faces and grease for the steam engines of Europe were being filled and checked. The oil came from plantations or wild palms up-river. The flesh of the date-like fruit was pulped and boiled to produce the oil. A further, laborious process of crushing the nuts yielded an oil of higher quality and price but often involved too much labour. It was better to ship them direct to Liverpool for processing. The Captain stood over the barrels himself, granitic and implacable as an angel at Judgement Day, checking for adulteration with water or tampering with the size of the containers. The history of trade on the Coast was one of mutual deception and dislike punctuated by outbursts of short but extreme violence.

His was one of the last vessels to trade under the old system, where captains dealt individually with the Africans on an *ad hoc* basis. They would simply arrive with a mixed cargo, which would be advanced to African traders on credit. Only the Africans were allowed to go to the inland markets to exchange the goods for other commodities. They were very firm in their resistance to all attempts to undermine their position as middle-men. White men who went inland tended not to return. On the other hand, white traders had scotched attempts by the Africans to ship their own produce direct to Europe. An uneasy *modus vivendi* had been arrived at by tacit consent: the Africans would ship through the Europeans; the Europeans would buy through the Africans. A grudging marriage of convenience that, unlike the Truscots', had never grown to a love match, since both partners had an eye to better offers.

Until recently the primary export had been slaves for the American plantations, the notorious cargoes described on the manifest as 'ebony'. With the embargo operated by the British West Africa Squadron and the enforcement of anti-slavery treaties by an increasingly belligerent British consul, that trade had become unprofitable. Only a few piratically desperate European and Brazilian slaving vessels were prepared to risk running the gauntlet on the Coast. Most limited their activities to 'legitimate' trade in vegetable products, oil, gums and rubber. They would simply roof over their vessels against the elements and batten down the hatches for a few months until the traders returned from the interior with their goods. But waiting on this pestilential coast was the most dangerous part. Few ships escaped without victims to the fever. Many lost as much as half their crew. Seamen would linger in fitful health down in the Delta only to perish on the voyage home, which should have restored them. The first two weeks homeward bound were especially dangerous, with many a flag-bound bundle tumbled into the waves off the Canaries. Even the sharks recognized the line. They followed home-bound ships, waggish as dolphins, for the first two weeks only, before turning their noses back to the Coast.

Most trade these days was done by permanent traders for big British companies. They would install themselves on dismasted, roofed-over sailing ships down in the creeks like nautical gypsies. These hulks would be linked to the land by a flimsy causeway that could be severed in times of stress. The sea breezes protected the traders from the miasma rising from the swamps. More than a way of trading, the system reflected a whole philosophy of life, the traders' unstated but deeply rooted view of the African mainland as dangerous, unstable, hostile and to be engaged through a policy of minimal personal contact via recognized intermediaries.

Further supplies of imported goods were crammed into King Jack's sheds. From one protruded the end of a harmonium, exposed to the wind and rain. Another housed a blue-painted carriage.

The Reverend Truscot sniffed, 'This is a temple of Mammon, a man possessed by his possessions. I rather think a sermon on the lines . . .'

'Look!' Mary exclaimed. 'They must have horses here.'

There was a cough. Prince John Bull had returned. 'No, Missus, no horses. By the way, we had no word for such animals, so "horse" was called "white man's cow". Then, "carriage" became "white man's cow box". We brought some horses to Akwa, but they always died. So now slaves pull the carriage. They don't die as fast.'

'But that's terrible.'

Prince John Bull smiled politely. 'That slaves don't die is terrible?'

'No, no. The other thing, using the men.'

'Why is it terrible? Men carry goods to the inland peoples like horses. Men paddle canoes like your Liverpool steamships. Why should they not pull the King? Or perhaps you mean the word is terrible? Akwa men make many words like that. The second-hand clothes that come from Liverpool, we call them "white man done die".'

Mary looked confused. 'I don't rightly know, but it's terrible.'

He changed the subject. 'The King will be pleased to receive you if you will follow me.'

They struggled out of the room with as much difficulty as they had struggled in.

King Jack received us today. Civil enough though covered from head to toe with malodorous yellow clay and smoking a pipe whose fumes made poor Mary ill. Prince John Bull says this is 'country doctor', a remedy prescribed by the ju-ju king for his ills – which derive no doubt largely from his consumption of trade gin. Although it was but ten in the morning, the King offered us a mug each of squareface. Mary naturally declined. Although I am not strict teetotal, taking a little Cuthbertson's Quinine Tonic Wine for my health's sake, yet I abstained on the grounds of the hour and so that stimulants when needful might be more efficacious. The King took this ill, demanding why white men would not drink what white men had sold him. I replied coolly that I certainly had no hand in the selling of it and that in my view it would be far better if no one consumed strong waters – white men included. To this, he replied with an extraordinary statement. His drunkenness, he claimed, was the measure of his piety since everyone who offers on the shrines of the local gods must drink some of the gin there poured as a libation. Thus the sober man is the ungodly!

He promises to consider a site for our house. I preached to him at length concerning the death of Our Saviour, Jesus Christ, which he seemed not to comprehend, and called upon him to forsake the Devil, which he declined – invited us, however, to dine, which I accepted.

Social intercourse in the Delta was characterized by an etiquette that varied considerably from that current at the Court of St James. Owing to the absence of white women in Akwa, many of the trade gentlemen had entered into arrangements of greater or lesser formality with Akwa ladies or even emancipated slaves presented by King Jack. The act of emancipation was always carefully observed, for it was now illegal by treaty for British subjects to own slaves in Akwa. Marriage, of course, was done without benefit of clergy, according to the flexible norms of Akwa custom. As King Jack summed these up, 'Wedding palaver no be big bob for we. We be all same two monkey in jungle.' In deference to the sex of Mrs Truscot and in defiance of Akwa norms of socialization, King Jack had strongly expressed his wish that these ladies should be present at court so that she should not be lacking fit company. He was certain Prince John Bull had maintained that white men took their women to their palavers. Indeed, he had known traders who took their dogs – so even so unlikely a thing was possible. Doubtless they were unsure of their virtue if left at home like those of Akwa men. Also in attendance were the chief traders to whom they were attached, enticed from their hulks for the evening not so much through deference to King Jack's wishes as from suspicion of any meeting at which they were not present. There was general embarrassment in the air at the enforced public declaration of liaisons that normally went deliberately unnoticed. Pasty white flesh sweated into cotton suits that bagged at crotch and elbow with damp. White protesting fingers ran round starched collars that dripped with moisture. African gentlemen wore either local or imported finery. Prince John Bull was resplendent in an immaculate but indelicately tight blue cavalry uniform complete with cocked hat and boots.

In the reception rooms of King Jack's iron castle all the doors were flung open but the heat was intense, as in a baker's oven after the bread has been taken out. Copious quantities of drink were mopped up by miserable and despairing guests. Reverend Truscot and Mary asked a servant for water. He shrugged incomprehension and brought them undiluted gin like everyone else. Mary looked around at the huge figures.

'Mannie, this is the first time I have ever thought of you as small. Amongst the Chinese you were a giant.'

'Amongst the Chinese, my dear, *you* were a giant.'

If the gentlemen were straitened by excess of dress, the ladies delighted in it. Many of the belles flaunted gowns that showed the latest trends from Sierra Leone couturiers – tight scarlet dresses of thin, glistening fabric with frilly, lacy bodices. Feathers blew to and fro at shoulders, flounces hung from exaggerated sleeves, fans clicked and whirred in a dozen hands. The more fashion-conscious ladies had imported the latest briar pipes from Liverpool to complete their ensembles. Mary gasped at the exaggerated bustles, then realized that these were no bustles but solid anatomy. Akwa taste favoured ladies of Junoesque proportions and behinds came equipped with a shelf on which books might have been kept. Young girls were consigned before marriage and after childbirth to compulsory inactivity and forced feeding in the fattening house, whence they emerged as featureless blobs and objects of erotic appreciation. Especially valued were the rings of fat around their necks, which wobbled when they walked. They wobbled quite a lot, the ladies being hobbled by having their wide toes crushed into unaccustomed shoes. They took immediately to Mary as a poor helpless creature, pitying her thin shoulders and dowdy, unbecoming frock. There was no rival here for the affections of their 'husbands'.

'Who are all these ladies, Mannie?'

'I don't know, my dear. I suppose they must be the wives of the African gentlemen.'

The ladies themselves considered Mary dispassionately.

'Indeed white ladies be very ugly.'

'She been ill, poor thing. It live for her face.'

'Her husband care nothing for her for that she barren.'

'Fault live for him, for sure. See he drink.'

'He too mean to fatten her.'

'Indeed white men be all same. All mine be.'

The matron of the Head of the River, mindful of her due position, led Mary to a seat and pressed her down gently into the musty fabric, plumping her fat bottom down beside her. The seat shuddered. She knocked back a glass of gin with a practised flick of the wrist and wiped her face with the gesture one would use in England to polish a mirror.

'My name Crashy Jane. How much your man pay for you?' She puffed smoke in Mary's face from an English briar.

Mary looked nervously around. Mannie was deep in conversation with the trader Crosby, head bent forward to catch what he was saying, eyes looking away. 'Nothing. In my country it is the custom for a wife to provide money and goods for herself on marriage.'

A scream of disbelief cut through the air and induced shocked silence.

'Child. You mean your family give money for *him*?'

'Er, yes. That is, we account it slavery for women to be bought and sold.'

'Slavery?' She roared, swaying to her feet. 'Slavery? How be it slavery if the man *pay*? That show respect. That show he not own her like a dog! I no be slave! Slavery!' She stalked off scandalized, her fan clicking erect like the tail of an outraged peacock.

'Oh dear!' Mary felt close to tears. She took a great draught of what she imagined was water and scorched her throat on raw potato spirit. Now her tears were real.

Truscot tried vainly to join her. His sleeve was seized by a fat man with pince-nez glasses, who spat as he talked.

'Slavery! Yes, indeed. You men of the cloth have views on *slavery*.' The accent was slight but clearly Germanic. Also hostile. 'Slavery is an integral part of African life, Father. You can't change human nature. There is slavery in every town and every village here. Europeans didn't invent slavery. They took it from Africa, but they changed it. The people serving drink here tonight, they're slaves. As the slave of a man, you're protected by him. Many of the richest Akwa traders are slaves or sons of slaves. Men find them less dangerous than their own blood. Slaves can have their own slaves. African slavery is quite unlike what you see on the American plantations. One must not be frightened of the word. It is more like adoption here, Father.'

Again, heat began to prickle under Truscot's collar. 'I am not of the Romish persuasion, therefore not a father. But is it not so, Mr . . . ?'

'Hauptmann. My name is Hauptmann.'

'Is it not so, Mr Hauptmann, that a master can kill his slave for any small offence if he wills it, that he has power of life or death and need answer to no man and no civil authority?'

'But it seldom happens. Slaves are valuable . . .'

'I have also heard that when a big chief dies, many slaves – aye, women and children, too – will be massacred to make a fitting end for him. According to my information, when the last king died, no less than two hundred poor souls were slain in conditions of the greatest suffering.'

Hauptmann pooh-poohed like a pigeon. 'Oh, no, not two hundred . . .'

'I have heard that many of these sad creatures are torn from their mother's breast in the interior, the milk yet wet upon their innocent lips, and plunged into degradation by their own family. You say slavery is based on the family; I would say that the family here is based on slavery, not the natural affections of men.'

Hauptmann opened his mouth to reply but a hand was slapped on his shoulder from behind, spilling his drink. A portly figure, who surely would have been red-faced in England but here mottled in shades of yellow, loomed over his shoulder.

'Slavery? No, it doesn't happen any more, Reverend. Good thing too.' He smirked smarmily. 'It was incompatible with the white man's role as a morally uplifting force. Sorry, let me introduce myself. Nash is the name. I'm Head of the River here. Lot of nonsense really, but the traders need a notional head to keep things on the proper footing. Bit like being School Captain.' He bared yellow fangs. 'What's Hauptmann been telling you? He doesn't like the English too much, you know.' A flash of the fangs was intended to take the edge off the remark but somehow only added malice.

'We were speaking of African slavery,' sulked Hauptmann.

'Ah yes. Different thing. As for the other sort, glad we stopped it. Always difficult and messy. All those cargoes labelled "ebony" turning up. That,' he explained, 'was what we used to put on the manifests, "ebony".'

'I thought it was the government in London that stopped it.'

'Eh? Ah, well. Yes, I suppose it was really. Or . . .' brightening, 'you might say that their passing the law enabled us to persuade our companies to do what *we* wanted to do anyway. Must give credit to you missionary chaps for pushing that one through.' He tapped Truscot on the lapel with his forefinger to convey congratulation.

Hauptmann snorted. 'How can you say slavery is abolished? What about the free emigration system?'

'What's that?' Truscot's nose, an old dog sniffing out sin, rose like a pointer's.

'Nothing,' said Nash hastily. 'Just a boring business palaver. Time for another drink perhaps.'

Hauptmann smirked, settling back on his heels as one launching into a major speech. 'We are no longer allowed to export our own slaves for sale, but there is no law against domestic slavery in Africa. What happens is that the Akwa men remain owners of the slaves but lease them to us for seven years so we can export them to work in the Jamaican plantations. In theory, at the end of seven years they return to Akwa and their legal owners, enlightened and enriched to the benefit of the country, but . . .' he shrugged, 'often they fail to return, so the owners here ask for a little bit extra, the whole price of a slave. But it is not slavery.'

'But this is dreadful! How long has this been going on? Does the British Consul know?'

Hauptmann made a distasteful expression. 'The British Consul has no legal right to intervene. King Jack is king of a sovereign country. Anyway, he is six days away in Fernando Poo and retires soon as the consul who ended slavery in Africa.'

'I shall write to my mission and the Colonial Secretary. This is insufferable hypocrisy.'

Nash's hand trembled around his tumbler of gin. 'It's the

same system the Krooboys have been using for years. Part of
Africa. There's slavery in the Bible, you know. It's only thanks
to us Europeans slaves were given their freedom at all. Don't
forget that about slavery. We didn't invent it. Leave well alone
for God's sake.'

'For God's sake! You make very free with the name of the
Deity, sir. It is for God's sake, man, that this must cease. Don't
you see that . . .'

Prince John Bull loomed up over Nash's shoulder, twinkling
amicably. 'You have met Mr Nash. Good, good. You are
shaking the hands of some of our familiar faces. Come, we must
eat.'

He seized Reverend Truscot under the armpit and conducted
him enthusiastically through a door into an iron gallery that ran
the length of the building. A series of long English tables had been
set end to end and decked with white linen. The tableware took no
study of the need for uniformity: a dozen different canteens of
cutlery had been mixed to deck it, many embossed with the
insignia of ships. A similar variety reigned amongst the glassware,
some guests being required to drink from small vases. Long
benches had been set against the tables and at the head sat King
Jack in his brass crown and on his accustomed European chair.

The European river gentlemen drifted into the room in a
wave of alcoholic disorder and loud chatter, lurched into their
seats on one side of the table and banged down their elbows,
oblivious to the presence of the King, who stared blankly
before him. Truscot found the Captain beside him and experienced that sinking feeling that comes to many a man's heart
when the identity of his dinner neighbour becomes known and
it is clear there can be no escape for hours. The African big
men of the kingdom installed themselves on the other side to
the accompaniment of grunts and groans as they settled their
massive frames. The benches creaked and sagged but held.

'My wife?' gasped Truscot, suddenly ashamed of forgetting her. 'Where is my wife?' King Jack scowled. Prince John Bull leant obligingly across the table.

'Why, Reverend Truscot, she will eat with the ladies. That is Akwa fashion.'

'Oh. I see.' In his mind's eye he saw poor Mary sitting in the baleful glare of Crashy Jane, her handkerchief gripped to her mouth in a gesture of nervous prostration.

Lesser figures crowded in behind the seated diners, crouching at their feet, and behind them scantily dressed servants (slaves? wondered Truscot) proffered brass bowls of water and towels. Truscot washed his face and hands, wiping himself gratefully on a towel. He could not forbear to look at it. It was stained with mud and sweat. The huge figure across from him leant forward. Truscot noted the sunken, piggy eyes and the enormous, undivided eyebrow that stretched across the forehead as though painted for amateur theatricals.

'I be Duke Bosun,' he rasped, 'brother for King Jack.' He poured liquid from a china water jug into Truscot's vase and deliberately tipped some on the ground. 'To cool the earth,' he explained soothingly. Truscot eyed the potation with caution, noting its turbid appearance and slight effervescence.

'What be – I mean – what is this?'

Duke Bosun turned to the others and made a remark in Akwa, the sound of water in a drain. There came a burst of laughter and they looked at Truscot smilingly.

'Palm wine, juice of palm tree. Don't worry, it no be strong. I think you be woman drinker.'

Truscot sipped tentatively and found it surprisingly pleasant despite a slightly fetid after-taste that would henceforth always be for him the quintessential smell of Akwa City. Food was borne in by more retainers, what Truscot already knew to be typical Akwa 'chop': soup, mashed yams and a mess of meat, prawns and fish soaked in palm-oil and ragingly hot pepper, all dishes to be eaten at the same time. Mashed yam was served in a container seldom seen above stairs. Truscot smiled and helped himself with a waggish gesture from a Staffordshire chamber-pot. It was excellent food. Servants bore round the jug, topping up as soon as a vase came empty. Truscot noted many of the Africans watching carefully the approach of the wine with gimlet eyes and a nervous licking of the lips. Their expressions recalled what he had seen in the faces of men coveting women in the Glasgow parish where he had first served: an unseemly mixture of greed and weakness.

The Africans fell on the food like wolves. Truscot noted that several of the European traders, too, ate with their fingers. That was perhaps mere deference to the social usages of Akwa, but he was scandalized that they followed the Akwa custom of throwing a pinch of every food on the floor before consuming it. That was pagan superstition – also bad hygiene. It occurred to him to attempt to say grace, but that could wait. Sooner delay the taste of ripe fruit than risk the bitterness of that precipitately plucked.

Occasionally they would pass morsels to those crouched at their feet, who might, in turn, pass them to others further from the table, a pleasing and democratic proceeding. Generally, however, it was only bones and gristle that fell to these latter. Truscot watched with awe as one cracked a large mutton bone – fit to frighten a dog – with his teeth and noisily sucked out the marrow.

'When *they* have finished,' remarked the Captain with satisfaction, 'what's left goes to the women. Slim rations for your wife I reckon.'

Duke Bosun spooned palm-oil on to his plate, forming a rich orange pool. He was clearly a long-distance eater, not one of your sprint feeders, able to wade steadily through a meal of infinite length by somehow balancing the amount ingested with the fuel his body used to consume it. Eating was an act that seemed to involve not only his hands and face but his whole body. He seemed less to eat the food than to move into the space it had occupied. Duke Bosun curled back his lips and showed oily teeth conversationally. 'I got Christian slave. He good boy. Plenty trade. Plenty money. He live for Bonny town, look after trade for me that place. Wife for him Christian too. Marry in white dress. He tell me white dress from Liverpool, cost plenty money – special ju-ju dress. I tell him, "You crazy chop money like that." Then, one, two day before he take woman she run for bush. So he take other woman in her place. She most ugly woman ever you saw but only one right size for dress.' He stared blankly at Truscot, then banged both his fists down on the table and uttered a bellow of laughter. 'I tell him better you throw dress and take fine woman.' He belched and broke wind stertor-ously, then leaned over to sniff his own product, but whether this was for aesthetic enjoyment or as some guide to his internal condition was impossible to say. A number of others replied with anal salvoes – some falsetto, mostly rumbling basses. Apparently, then, it was not impolite to do so in Akwa. Truscot shifted uncomfortably on thin buttocks, smiled weakly and turned his attention to the Captain, who was flexing and massaging his arm.

'Is your arm troubling you, Captain? Perhaps you would like my servant, Ali, to look at it. The Malays are very gifted in massage.' The Captain grunted. King Jack leant forward, dabbing at his mouth with his napkin in a curiously matronly fashion. 'He flog Krooboy,' he confided with awe in his voice. 'I see him from my castle. Flog him fine.' He shook his head in inexpressible admiration.

Again the prickling round Truscot's collar. 'That's barbarous! You flogged a man? What, pray, had he done? What fault so grievous that it merited so dreadful a punishment?'

The Captain looked at him wearily. 'Done? Why, he cost me near two hundred pound in gold, fell over the side while we were unloading today and lost the lot. Krooboys swim like fish, but the water there's too deep for any hope of recovery.'

He looked so exhausted that Truscot without thought began to comfort him. 'Riches grow wings and fly off like an eagle towards Heaven, Captain.'

'Aye, well these flew in quite another direction and without wings.'

'But let us give thanks that the Krooboy was spared.'

'It were better yet had he been lost and the money spared.'

Further down the table a bespectacled trader he recognized as Crosby, Prince John Bull's mentor, ducked forward to address the Reverend. 'Such is the nature of commerce on the Coast. The natives are careless, godless and a bunch of thieves. The only thing that keeps trade together is discipline.'

Truscot was struck by the way he could talk of Africans in this fashion before the King, as if he did not exist – as one would chatter in England before servants schooled to invisibility.

'They have no respect for us,' he continued wonderingly. 'They will even enslave a European if he falls among them. That's why we offer a premium to buy them back if they run aground round here. One poor fellow last year, a Spanish sea-captain, wrecked on a shoal near here and the natives came out in droves in their dug-outs. The poor man in his simplicity believed them to be hurrying to his rescue. Tore the ship apart, rigging, fittings, the rings in the deck. Stripped the very clothes off his back. Fortunately, they knew it was worth their while to sell the poor devil back to us. They have no sense of natural justice . . .'

'Rings in the deck? Whatever were there rings in the deck for?'

Nash stared at Truscot as at an imbecile. 'For the *slaves*, man. What do you think? The Spanish still operate along the Coast.' Nash went into an extended coughing fit.

Somewhere a chicken screeched. Clearly one had wandered into the room and Truscot looked down about his feet, seeking it there. King Jack scratched petulantly under his shirt and the head of a chicken briefly appeared as in some conjuring trick, to be thrust back again. Truscot found it hard to mask his astonishment, while the Captain giggled in a fashion like to set the hair on end of those that knew him. The Reverend felt giddy. Perhaps it was the palm wine or simply the comprehensive madness of the evening. The bowls and towels came round again, cooling his hot face.

'And now,' said Nash with provocative relish, 'cards.'

The tables were cleared and groups formed, ignoring Truscot. Europeans and Africans played at separate tables. He watched with horror as the calling cards of the Devil were distributed. King Jack took his seat with a large thigh bone by his place. 'This be fetish for me,' he explained obligingly and thumped it on the cloth. Many of the traders had their own lucky pieces, Koranic amulets, silver coins that they rubbed before dealing, large polished nuts. The servants came round with brandy, which Truscot, isolated without a table, declined. 'Right,' Nash articulated loudly, 'let's not just play for money. Let's have a little fun. One sovereign to represent one slave. I bet two slaves.' A snort of derisive laughter ran round the table. People stole glances at him. He knew this to be a deliberate affront, a cocking of snooks at divine truth and decency.

He rose trembling to his feet. 'King Jack, I thank you for your hospitality this night. I don't know where you could have learned such good manners considering the company you are forced to keep. If you will have the goodness to show me to my wife, we will take our leave of you and return to the ship. I beg you to reflect on the matter of our house. I do not wish to impose any longer than strictly necessary on the good grace of the trading gentlemen.'

Concern was writ large over King Jack's face. He hesitated, unsure of his manners, scratched at the chicken under his shirt, then motioned to Prince John Bull, who rose reluctantly from the gaming table and led the Reverend to the door. The traders snickered like schoolboys who had inflicted a humiliation on a master. As they strode down the iron corridor, he heard Nash's voice bray out.

'Spades are trumps! My hand, I think!'

When the Truscots had reached the end of the corridor and were safely out of earshot, Nash turned to the King, suddenly serious.

'About their house. It would not, I think, be wise to refuse it. There is the treaty you signed with the *Rattler* and it would look bad to the Consul and his men-of-war. It would be *much* better if they were to simply become discouraged. I have, Majesty, a suggestion . . .'

King Jack nodded dumbly. How very rude that God-man was. He had not even broken wind before leaving.

Much restored from my despair of yesterday. Mary is no longer ill from, I am sure, purgative excess of palm-oil. The Lord casts us down and he lifts us up again. Yesterday I had word that the King has granted us land on a fine promontory just outside the town. I have visited it with Prince John Bull and find it not subject to inundation and salubrious. We have already engaged Krooboys and are unloading the house and goods we brought from Liverpool. Soon our business shall be set on foot and our paths made straight. The Krooboys eagerly begged for copies of the Lord's word even though they cannot read.

The Reverend Truscot was active in his supervision of building works. Where the Krooboys were unfamiliar with an operation, he would explain it to them exhaustively, drawing diagrams in the soil with a stick. Where they claimed familiarity, he taught them at even greater length, convinced that all change under his direction must be counted improvement. He constantly reproved their strong language. Mary rested quietly in the shade, recovering from the prostration caused by their attendance at court and writing letters to friends in England. She was not discontent. At last, after all the false starts, they had broken the first soil of God's new field. The enemy had been identified and engaged. Above all, she had faith in Mannie as the tempered instrument of God. As his wife, she would follow him anywhere. Ali brought her cool water, boiled and chilled.

'Thank you, Ali. How do you like Akwa, Ali?' He blushed as he always did when she addressed him unexpectedly.

'Less Chinese I reckon than in Singapore. One good thing.'

A space some forty feet square had been cleared at the very top of the hill. From here, they commanded both Akwa City and the whole roadstead, with all its European vessels riding at anchor. The Reverend Truscot was instructing the workers how best to drive in the mangrove poles that would be the house's foundation. They had been driving in mangrove poles since they could walk. God's children would not build upon sand. As they toiled, the Krooboys intoned a rhythmic chorus that seemed a song of creation. The muscles on their shoulders stood out like ropes. Sweat flowed copiously.

'Why does your father wear a chicken under his shirt?' asked Ali. 'Is it a pet?' He had once owned a pet monkey that picked coconuts for him and even slept entwined around his waist. He tucked his feet up comfortably inside his sarong. He was delighted to see that Akwa men wore them too.

Prince John Bull laughed. 'No. The ju-ju king told him to. It is Akwa fashion. If someone tries to make you ill, you tie the chicken next your body. Then *it* gets ill in your place. You hear how much it complains? That is because of all the illness it soaks up. It is like the socks on your feet.' Ali frowned. He did not wear socks.

'Who is trying to make him ill?'

'Who knows? To tell, you have to make them chop nut – eat a nut that kills them if they are guilty of "freemason" – witchcraft. They vomit if they are innocent. That is the only sure way to tell. Maybe it is the traders. Maybe Duke Bosun. Maybe even your master.' He looked at Ali expectantly.

Ali was accustomed to the inexplicable malice of fellow villagers. At home they would creep under the house at night to bury medicine that made a man's member weak or a woman sterile. But white men, though often cruel, simply did not know how to do these things. 'No. It is not my master. He only prays to God. He knows nothing of freemason. I have watched him carefully.'

'Yes, I know, white men cannot be freemason. But your master is a ju-ju man. He must have powers. Why do you stay with him? You say his God is not your God and white men are strange, they will not let other men have the gods they choose.'

'He is a good man. He cured me once when I was sick. He helps me when my family are in trouble. In many ways he is both my father and my child. I must look after him.' He was embarrassed at such a frank avowal and began to pick at his sockless feet.

'Then perhaps he should wear a chicken under his shirt, for people will surely try to kill him.'

Ali flexed his toes experimentally. 'He would not do that. He would call it "magic" and that is bad. Is there no way we can protect him?'

Prince John Bull smiled. 'We can make him ju-ju, blow Ekpo over him. Then anyone who harms him must die the Ekpo death.'

'How would the people know he was ju-ju?'

'An Ekpo runner would go round the town with a bell. Also, we would carve the Ekpo mark by his door so all would know.'

'How much would it cost? I have little money.'

'How much can you pay? You must borrow something from your master. He is a rich man and it is for him that you are doing this thing. Give me six copies of their ju-ju book.'

'What will you do with them, my friend?'

'The Krooboys buy them to make charms, or they rub salt on them and swear their labour contracts. Also they are exactly the right size to make the wadding when we load our Daneguns. It is said that only with such wadding can you shoot a white man. It is only fool fashion.'

'Why would you wish to shoot a white man?'

Prince John Bull shrugged. 'Who can say? Who can know? I am not God.'

'I will do it.' They reached forward and clicked their fingers together.

'That's good, brother Ali. You may as well go the whole hog and be hanged for the sheep not the lamb.'

Our house rises relentlessly from the black soil, an unusual structure for Akwa in that every vertical line *is* vertical and every horizontal unflinchingly flat. King Jack's iron house alone has this same peculiarity. The Krooboys all hastened to present their 'characters', references carefully preserved in wooden boxes and sealed with gum against damp and termites. Many previous employers had taken advantage of their ignorance of letters to indulge their own vituperative propensities. 'Big Monty is the laziest bounder it has ever been my misfortune to employ. I advise any potential master to bethink himself again.'

'Blackface Tom is a master of all the arts of idleness but has a quite special gift for drunkenness.' These, of course, were all tendered with simple pride.

I left the carpenters to their work and went to town on business. When I returned, they had all departed the house and were nowhere to be found. I sent word to their quarters that I should not pay a full day's pay for such neglect of their duties. They sent a spokesman who apologized to such good purpose and made so many fair promises that I repented of my rash harshness. The following morning I again left them at their work and, returning at noon, found they had abandoned the site completely. When I again sent word to them as before, they claimed to be amazed and uncomprehending at my complaint, yet made the same fair promises as on the previous day. What can one do? Mr Crosby sees in this the proof that Africans may not be trusted and are doomed to be eternally inferior to white men. I see in this the proof that they are every bit like workmen at home.

In order to minimize their moral debt to the Captain, Reverend Truscot and Mary moved on to the site as soon as walls were standing. A tarpaulin stretched over them assured cover in case of rain and shade in the heat of the day. Ali prepared food in a Dutch oven, a simple dustbin buried in hot ash, further cinders being shovelled over the lid. It was like an extended picnic. Truscot had never taken Mary on a picnic when they were courting. For the first time it began to feel like an adventure.

Truscot lay awake at night listening to the sounds of the water and the wind, the regular slosh and trickle of the small eddies on the river, the more distant boom and hiss of the surf. Fireflies skittered about the site like miniature stars. The air was hot and humid. Somewhere a dog barked. They had just discharged their marital duties for the first time on African soil, it being a Thursday. By unspoken arrangement this always occurred on Thursday, as that was the day of the week on which they had been married. The act was always preceded by a prayer adapted from the grace. Afterwards, they adjusted their dress and kneeled to give thanks for what they had received. Truscot was swift, efficient, as though putting up a shelf. Mary slept contentedly, having performed the office of a good wife. One good thing about Mannie: in sexual matters he was a good husband and never bothered her unduly.

A furtive scuffling grated on his nerves. Thieves? They had not unloaded their stores. There was nothing much to steal, a few supplies in the kitchen perhaps. The answer came in a flash. It was one of those cursed iguanas. He pictured its leathery neck extending as it plunged its head into the sugar and flour in the kitchen, saw its clumsy clawed feet strewing the tea over the dirt. Very well. He rose quietly, girding up his dressing gown and took a shoe in his hand, testing its hard sole against his palm. Sacred to Akwans they might be, but there was no one to take offence at this hour. Silently, he tiptoed to the end of the wall, his eyes adjusting slowly to the moonlight. The fresh timber glowed in the pale light, the knots standing out like swirls of smoke. He took a deep breath, leapt around the corner with a great cry and raised the shoe to strike.

In what was to be the living room stood an elephant. It stared at him in demure surprise, then raised its trunk and ran it around the walls like a mistress checking the picture rail for dust. Truscot felt no fear. He looked at the shoe and began to laugh. From his schooldays, indeed all his life, he had been punished for his overdeveloped sense of the absurd. Ali appeared behind him tying the waist of his sarong, pattering on flat feet.

'Wah! *Tuan. Alangkah besarnya gajah itu!*'

'Very big,' agreed Truscot. 'Perhaps we should ask it to leave.' There was a moment of embarrassment, as if they did not know where to put their hands. Ali flapped his sarong fitfully in the way he would chase away a cat. Truscot shouted 'Begone!' in exorcism.

The elephant observed them impassively, then swung round as if departing in a huff. There was a ripping of timber as it struck the side wall. Surprised, it looked round and its trunk smashed into the opposite wall. For a moment everything was held in abeyance and then, slowly, inexorably, the walls dipped and crashed outwards. The elephant paused as if shocked by the enormity of the effect, as one pauses to survey a dropped vase or a shattered window, feeling the result to be too sudden, too severe.

'Heaven preserve us!'

The walls now having been laid low, as the dust cleared, a large crowd of further spectating elephants could be seen observing the events with serious and detached interest. Mary emerged, fuddled by sleep and rubbing her eyes. Already she was fussing with her hair. He felt a twinge of paternal affection.

'Mannie,' she asked innocently, puzzled by the shoe in his hand, 'why have you done this?'

'It was not I,' he retorted hotly. 'It was the elephants.'

'Elephants?' Mary became aware of them for the first time and uttered a squeal.

'Don't worry, *ibu*. They are not dangerous!' Ali looked at Truscot. 'But I think we have to move the house.'

'But why, Ali?'

'This must be a path the elephants use. Always they follow the same trails down to the water to bathe. They never change. Same back home. You can't move the trail and plant your fields or build your house. You must respect it. They will just keep coming back. The only choice is to kill them all.'

'Is there no alternative?' Mary looked around her sadly.

'Only to use a *bomoh* doctor to ask the elephants to leave.'

'Magic, Ali,' Truscot said grimly.

Ali shrugged. 'Magic? Only if anything you cannot explain or do yourself is magic.' He rounded on Truscot and waved a finger at him. 'You use an interpreter to talk to a Chinese. Why is it wrong to use a *bomoh* to talk to the elephants? If you wanted to give orders to a Chinese elephant, you would use a Chinese driver. *That* would be all right. Why is the other different?' It was a matter they had often discussed before.

'Because . . . because an elephant is not a Chinaman.' Even to him it sounded silly. He and Ali began to laugh.

'Well,' said Mary, baffled by their absorption in rough-hewn philosophy, 'I suppose it is no more work to begin again just a little bit along the coast, rather than put up the house again here to be knocked down every night by elephants. Come along, Mannie. Back to bed.'

As they rebuilt their bedding in a somewhat reduced shelter a puzzled rhinoceros stopped to watch.

The renewed building operations did not lack human spectators, so that the first and most essential part of the structure was a stout fence to keep them back. Many brought supplies and several enterprising ladies opened food stalls to supply the needs of the improvident. Prince John Bull was faithful in his attendance, showing himself cheerfully helpful in all circumstances. On the other hand, the Reverend Truscot was never a man to waste either time or an audience and hastened to enlighten his gazing flock on the fundamentals of Divine Law.

'Prince John Bull, I wonder if you would be so kind as to assist me by translating to these good people by the fence.'

Mary looked worried. 'Mannie, is this wise? Surely the proper time is when the school is built.'

'My dear, the school is made for Man, not Man for the school.' She bowed her head meekly.

The Prince smiled obligingly and advanced to the boundary, Truscot following a pace behind. He took a deep breath and seized his lapels with both hands. 'You're all damned!' he cried.

The Prince looked blank. A woman's mouth gaped open in astonishment.

'They're all damned *what*, Reverend?' Truscot let out his breath. This was a sermon he had last used on the poor of Glasgow, but he could see that it might not work here. What else was there in stock? The sermon he had used at the local boys' school? – 'Carnal pleasure outside the wedded state is like a pair of football boots, all very well in themselves but, without the spirit of the game, lacking in meaning.' No, that would not do either. He tried a different tack.

'The Lord God has vouchsafed his laws unto us.' The Prince paused, then shrugged and began to rumble and bark a translation in the local tongue. People looked up from their food, intrigued. A man chewing a stick approached the fence and lent on it with one elbow, the way that in England one would contemplate a pig in a field.

'If you honour these laws and cherish them in your hearts, yours will be the Kingdom of Heaven.'

'Sorry, Reverend. The Kingdom of Heaven is a place ruled by the white queen of Liverpool?'

'No, no, Prince John Bull. The Kingdom of Heaven is . . . is the castle of God.'

'Ah . . .' The Prince resumed his rumbling. The man by the fence frowned and paused in his mastication.

'Thou shalt have none other gods before me.'

'You must not worship other ju-jus in front of my house.'

'Thou shalt not make thee any graven image or any likeness of any thing that is in heaven above – God's castle – or that is in the earth beneath or that is in the waters beneath the earth: thou shalt not bow down thyself unto them nor serve them.'

'You must not copy God's goods or the things he keeps for fancy – his hats and clothes or his pictures. You must not bow down to God like you do in Ekpo.'

'Thou shalt not take the name of the Lord thy God in vain, for the Lord will not hold him guiltless that taketh his name in vain.'

'Whenever you swear hot oaths, you must use God's name, for you will never do so in vain. So always use his name for your swearing.'

'Keep the Sabbath day to sanctify it, as the Lord thy God hath commanded thee. Six days shalt thou labour and do all thy work, but the seventh is the Sabbath of the Lord.'

'He says you must work six days without rest. You must not stop even if you be tired or God will hate you.'

'Honour thy father and thy mother, as the Lord thy God hath commanded thee; that thy days may be prolonged and that it may go well with thee in the land which the Lord thy God giveth thee.'

'Set up ju-ju for your father and mother or they will have the right to kill you or sell you as a slave abroad.'

'Thou shalt not kill.'

'He says it is not good to kill too many people. Indeed he speaks truly. To do so is wasteful. They could be sold as slaves instead.'

'Neither shalt thou commit adultery.'

'You women must stop all your sleeping with men other than your husband.'

'Neither shalt thou steal.'

'You must stop your taking of the goods of traders and not paying for them.'

'Neither shalt thou bear false witness.'

'If people are lying all the time, you must not carry them in your canoes. Only honest people may you carry about the country.'

'Neither shalt thou desire thy neighbour's wife, neither shalt thou covet thy neighbour's house, his field or his man-servant, or his maidservant, his ox or his ass, or any thing that is thy neighbour's.'

'Do not just sit there and feel lust for your neighbour's wife or want any of his goods. Ask God's help and they will all be yours. This is certain.'

The people clapped and roared, throwing back their heads. This was a novel theology and one that was welcome to them. They crowded forward and pressed Truscot's hand between theirs. Truscot was more than pleased at his reception, smiling triumphantly at Mary.

'Tell them to come here again. Tomorrow we open our school that all may learn of the path to Heav . . . God's castle.'

At last, today, we drove the first furrow in this new field of endeavour. A large number of people came to the house, though many, I fear, from idle curiosity rather than religious zeal. The ladies particularly were assiduous in opening all the doors and inspecting all the cupboards. One must work slowly to wean a tiger's cubs to gentler sustenance.

I begin to have high hopes of Prince John Bull. He is invaluable as interpreter and diligent in his studies as well as generous in his help of others. Already he is literate, though better versed in figures than in letters. He has arranged for me to hire two of King Jack's servants at very moderate cost to help with domestic labours since Mary is occupied in teaching dressmaking, though it must be confessed that thus far Eve's dress is the ladies' favoured wear.

One tragic and grievous event marred this day and curtailed our scholastic labours. Ali rushed into the classroom in great excitement to say that a corpse had been left against our door. I went out to look for myself and, indeed, there lay the body of an old man – quite naked and bound to a carrying pole but, God be thanked, bearing no signs of violence. I had the servants come from King Jack carry it away and bury it, though at first they refused. I cannot understand why they should leave the dead man here. Perhaps he was yet alive when left before the door and expired before we could bring him aid? Moving about the town I have noticed that I am followed everywhere by a small silent youth, who walks some three paces behind me like a dutiful wife. He does not approach me, asks for nothing, yet if I am in a building, he sits quietly before the door and patiently awaits my return. It is probably mere curiosity and will wear off as my newness becomes tarnished.

The school prospered. Akwa parents could scarce believe that the Reverend Truscot was prepared to teach their young to read and write without payment, skills bought and sold dearly in Akwa. They perhaps failed to realize that literacy was a sprat to catch a mackerel.

Reverend Truscot was increasingly troubled by the state of nudity of his pupils. What was especially troubling was that the pupils – like Adam and Eve – had no awareness of their nakedness. He explained the nature of his concern to Prince John Bull, whom he, in turn, lectured on the grounds of excessive dandyism. The Prince was confused.

'Do you want me to go naked like a pulla-boy? It no be fit I dress like a wolf in cheap clothing.'

'No, no, no, John Bull. Human improvement is intimately connected with clothing, which ministers both to the moral feelings and personal comfort, as well as elevating the wearer in social position. I think that *you* should concern yourself a little less with niceties of dress and the rest of the populace rather more.'

John Bull picked pensively on his teeth with a small stick, the end chewed into a brush. 'Perhaps, Reverend. But consider. Is it better that they go naked and take pride in clean bodies or wear the filthy rags of the towns such as Bonny where there are missionaries? My people believe that such clothing is insanitary and causes a weakening of the body. You will see that the people here have clean skins and no sores. Those of Bonny are hideous through scabs and festering wounds.'

The Reverend scratched absently at a sore developing under his gaiter. 'Nonsense. What of shame? It is not fitting that each should view the other in their entirety. It is an incitement to wickedness and inflames the immoral propensities of the young, which may be but scarcely held in check.'

'But here we believe the other, Reverend Truscot. It is nudity that sorts the sheep from the oats. It is the shrouding of nakedness that excites. If a girl puts on clothes, it must mean that she is seeking to hide something from her mother, who will know thereby that she has taken a lover. Here if a girl ceases to be a virgin, the whole town knows at once. Is it not so in Liverpool?'

Reverend Truscot smiled kindly. 'Poor Prince John Bull. You have much to learn. It is also extremely bad that the girls here deck themselves with jewels and ornament, making hideous that which God made beautiful.'

The Prince picked carefully round a molar and swilled around the root with his tongue. He pointed the stick at Truscot accusingly. 'But to cut one's hair, to shave, is that not interference in God's plan? This you do.' He considered Truscot's wild and neglected hair with distaste. 'Anyway, it is only married ladies who wear ornament. Young girls must go naked till their husbands dress them.'

This would not do. Having no toothbrush to hand, Truscot tinkled the chain of his fob-watch. 'A wife who seeks to charm her husband only, need not descend to the harlotry of ornament. It is a sure mark of one who tends away from the stony path of virtue and forbearance, an incitement to immorality, so that a woman may not pass about the town at night and know her honour safe.'

'But Reverend, this is not so. Only the wives of great chiefs, big, powerful traders, can afford the decorations of which you speak. All Akwa men know that you may attempt any woman but the wives of these. They would have your head. We have a saying, "The sound of a head rolling in the dirt is the sound of a brass anklet jingling."'

'Prince John Bull. You are very far from God!'

They were disturbed by a loud altercation from outside. Hurrying out, the Reverend Truscot was amazed to disturb two large fellows engaged in depositing a dead person in the middle of his living room. The deceased appeared to have succumbed to a hideous bloating disease.

'Stop it! Stop this at once!' He attempted to prevent their exit by interposing himself between them and the door, but they smiled politely, stepped round him and retired at their leisure.

'Prince John Bull!' The Prince entered the room looking furtive and revolving his straw hat guiltily in his hands.

'Prince John Bull. I feel sure you must understand what is happening here. Please be honest with me and explain.' The Reverend looked tired and drawn. Prince John Bull stared fixedly at his boots.

'This is the "bad bush",' he muttered softly.

Truscot drew himself up with dignity. 'What, pray, is the "bad bush"?'

'When a man dies a bad death – of freemason or dies before his own father, or sometimes when a woman dies in childbirth – then we bring them to the bad bush. They cannot be buried with other people. It would annoy the goddess of the earth. They are left here to be eaten by the crabs and the creatures of the bush. It is our custom.' He looked earnestly at Truscot.

The Reverend closed his eyes and breathed deeply. 'So, then, it amounts to this. Your father has given us space to live amongst the abominations of the earth and assigned us the place of the diseased and the dead of ill-omen. We are classed with that which is vile and hateful to Akwa men.'

Prince John Bull looked miserable and hunched-up like a small child engaged in some vile and private act in a room on which the door had suddenly been flung open. 'Yes, Reverend,' he said quietly. 'It was Mr Nash's idea.' The normal excuse of a child caught in wickedness. Truscot could see shame writ large over that usually cheerful mien. 'Shame,' he thought, 'is the offspring of the acknowledgement of sin and wrongdoing. Through this ill deed the Lord has brought this young man to a finer understanding of what is right and what he owes to himself. I shall save him. This I now know with certainty.' Silently, he bowed his head in what Prince John Bull took to be despair but was, in fact, celestial triumph.

A disturbed night. Held a long counsel with Mary and Prince John Bull, coming finally to the conclusion that we should forsake this place and seek another for our house. But it was not to be. The Lord taketh, yet he giveth again also. In the early morning, while it was still yet dark, the entire household was roused by Ali rushing around the yard shouting delightedly, 'Babies! Little babies!' He had been roused by noises and feared tigers, attracted by the carrion of this place. But lo! No tigers, only two abandoned infants, twin boys, left naked and helpless inside the fence. Inquiries reveal that it is the Akwa custom to pitilessly expose twins in the bad bush, the people holding them an abomination. The women are believed guilty of intercourse with wild beasts and punished by being driven from the town, eking out a miserable existence in the swamps and forest, where they may be preyed on and even killed with impunity. Yet they yearn desperately for children and barrenness is frequently grounds for putting away a wife. Here we see the working of the adage that 'oft God punishes Man by giving him that which he most earnestly desires.'

The children we have named James and John (they could not both be Moses!) and we take them as a sign that our work is to civilize the 'bad bush', not to flee from it. So here we shall stay. Prince John Bull is greatly afraid of the twins and will not approach them, yet he has found a Sierra Leone woman who is prepared to nurse them. I note that they are unusually pale for the denizens of this area, which leads me to think their genitor may be a trader. Prince John Bull, however, says that all Akwa children are so at birth and become black only through exposure to the rays of the sun, suggesting that the children of Ham were once white.

Prince John Bull, perceiving perhaps our dismay at his duplicity, kindly ornamented our doorway and the gate with carvings executed by his own hand. These were not lacking in skill and showed rudiments of taste. The local people even seemed greatly in awe of them.

Scarce had we recovered from the alarums and excursions of the night when we heard a thunder of guns from the river. Looking down, we perceived an English man-of-war firing off what must have been sixty-eight pounders. Ali, who gathers his intelligence I know not where, declared this to be the British Consul for the Delta, Humphrey Scuttlebutt, long expected for 'heavy trade palaver'. I fear he must be a man greatly given to ostentation to arrive with such a hallooing and beating of the nautical chest. It would be politic, however, to see him as quickly as possible before our enemies can enmesh him in their intrigues.

The silent youth who dogs my steps sleeps, it seems, by the gate. He will not approach when called and if I advance, he retreats. He is doubtless one of the poor dispossessed souls of this town. Perhaps he is mad. I have told Ali to leave food for him.

Humphrey Scuttlebutt, Her Britannic Majesty's Consul for the West Coast, hoped very soon to become *Sir* Humphrey Scuttlebutt. A man who felt the full dignity of his fifty-odd years, he had risen to his present low eminence by a policy unique in the British navy – that of not making waves. His stance had been one of steadfast vacillation, ubiquitous absence and deliberate vagueness. Through this, he had been promoted from ship's surgeon to diplomatic orderly in this backwater of empire, never having been firmly identified with any particular party or any difficult cause.

In as far as the British government had a policy in the area at all, it was as vague as Humphrey Scuttlebutt's natural inclinations might have wished, being definable as 'the protection and promotion of British interests'. It had never been realized in Whitehall that British interests were far from forming a single, self-evident and consolidated entity. The merchants wished the Consul to restrain foreign competition and to rap on the doors of the Africans, calling in debts while entirely freeing trade from any legal and moral obligations. He was only too aware that those who howled their need of protection from hostile natives were those who had sold them guns and powder in the first place. The Africans, who had little say in the matter, having no powerful lobby in England, sought to use the Consul as a sort of school prefect to restrain the traders, but otherwise disdained his incursion into their sovereignty. The missionaries desired him to exercise control over local despotism and moral excesses among both traders and natives, to be the muscle in the hand of God. The navy required him to leave them severely alone to cruise the healthier southern waters with enough opportunity for engagements with slavers of inferior armament to ensure rapid promotions. At all costs, they wished to be spared the necessity of visiting muddy, pestilential creeks with their haughty keels.

Then there was the problem of the various colonies established along the Coast by the European powers, including Britain – the constant bickering with local governors over relative jurisdictions. In such circumstances Humphrey became used to the fact that the slightest action on his part raised howls of protest from one party, if not all parties, while inaction could always be blamed on orders from above. It seemed, therefore, best to do very little and allow larger policy matters to simply wash him flotsam-like from event to event. By inertia and acquiescence he finally became identified in Whitehall as the man who, alone and with ruthless energy, had totally suppressed the slave trade on the Coast. Honours would surely follow.

There is a rule by which all public institutions gradually evolve so as to be run for the exclusive benefit of those that work within them and take no account of any direct external purpose. Thus it was with the consulship. Humphrey saw its justification not in terms of doing, but more as simply being. When pressed, he would speak, vaguely again, of his role in 'the exercise of moral force'. Privately, in a rare *bon mot*, he admitted that moral force without a man-of-war was moral farce, and, to the extreme irritation of the West Africa Squadron, had ensured the right to commandeer their vessels for purposes of transport and enforcement. Under his orders he also had two hundred Hausa troops of good military stamp, who combined the local relish for a fine brawl with the rudiments of conditioned discipline. His reluctant interventions were for the most part less the result of mature, senatorial reflection than of sudden bursts of irritation. The British lion was enraged by the plaguing mosquito states of the Coast and wont to lash out immoderately.

The school is the institution by which, for the rest of their lives, the British come to understand all arbitrary authorities of capricious brutality. It was in such terms that Humphrey saw his own position. He was quite simply a headmaster. He remembered those figures, awesome, remote and unapproachable, from his childhood. Normally, they would hold themselves aloof on a higher plane of being. On rare occasions they would descend to reward a favoured pupil – one, for example, who affected to find humour in Martial or beauty in Virgil. More frequently, they would appear in the grip of a terrible and disproportionate wrath to mete out incomprehensible punishment for unsuspected sins. Such was Humphrey's accustomed role on the Coast. He would arrive, unexpectedly, in towering rage at some rather habitual atrocity committed on the person of a British subject. Possibly a local ruler had withheld due payment for goods or flirted with foreign traders. Very occasionally, barbarous customs prohibited by treaty had been revived. To mark such happenings Humphrey would, headmaster-like, impose fines and banishments. Once he had burnt a village, twice fired over a town to ensure compliance with his demands. It was all lines, house-points or six of the best to him.

He looked out over the steamy river from his cool spot on the after-deck, shaded under a canvas awning, sailors pattering deferentially to attend to his every need in a rustle of white cotton. Idly, he drew a little pattern with his toe in the white lead insect killer that covered the deck. He nursed an early-morning snifter comfortably against his paunch and stroked his moustache contentedly. He was what Reverend Truscot would term 'a lover of the smooth things of life'.

There was the *Ethiope* again, her roof half finished. There were the traders' hulks. Some looked a little more seedy, a trifle lower in the mud than last season. The iron on Crosby's roof was beginning to rust. In the navy it would be scraped and repainted, but traders bothered little with such things. Beneath the water the worms were boring and the barnacles encroaching. Soon the hulk would be abandoned and in a few seasons only large bleached timbers, too heavy to be removed by the natives, would remain. Humphrey yawned with relish. A bit like the new English clerks really. Young lads, their death warrants written in their faces, lured out with the promise of £60–100 a year, not realizing that most of them would be long dead before their first payment was due. Most employees of the companies never lived to collect their pay. Good business, that.

He watched small boats and canoes plying between the vessels and the shore, many bearing ensigns of ludicrous size, so that they dragged in the water. His attention was seized by one proceeding rapidly but in strange fits and starts. The boatman seemed surprisingly light-hued and was rowing in a curious, oriental standing position. The passenger was tall and fierce-looking, in the costume of a cleric. But it was the face that captured Humphrey's attention. He looked just like a headmaster.

The mystery of the silent youth is solved. He is Will, a poor creature of King Jack's household assigned to me as a way of getting rid of him and too shy to approach me. So be it. He looks strong and willing. I have instructed Ali to set him to work. I call him Silent Will.

Delayed this morning by seeking out the mother of James and John before departing to visit the Consul. Mary being ill with a bad cold, I went alone. I was led to her in a pitiful hovel outside the town. She showed no gratitude that I had saved her offspring – indeed she reviled me as one perpetuating the memory of her shame. Thus it is in all nations that reverence for old fashions and old custom rules more than reason or Divine Authority and that mothers grow worse than tigers to devour their own young.

Ali conducted me to the vessel of Consul Scuttlebutt, riding in the harbour. Almost certainly a fool, yet attended the short Divine Service I held aboard the ship, to which the captain readily had assented. I took advantage of the presence of a ship's surgeon for treatment of a sore on my leg. A Scot. He advised me to keep it open and said that he would fain have availed himself of my religious services but that Calvinist scruples did prevent it. So I arose as I was and stamped out saying that, in that case, my own scruples prevented my using *his* services.

The Hausa troops are revealed to be Muslims from the north, so that Ali, too, experienced the joy of entering the community of his faith. I spoke of the need to honour the Sabbath – concerning which the captain of the vessel spoke most sensibly and the Consul at great length and to no purpose. One of the officers remarked privately that in his days as a ship's surgeon, the Consul was known as slow to give treatment but swift to amputate. Let us hope he has changed. During our return, an adventure.

Ali turned round, mouth agape, at the shot, dropping one of the oars. From Crosby's hulk came a loud shouting and cursing followed by several heavy splashes. A number of black figures were in the water. It seemed that several of Crosby's Krooboys were in pursuit of a lone swimmer, who was making off with powerful strokes, churning the brown river like a dreadnought. Crosby stood at the stern and fired wildly at the figure. Truscot directed Ali towards them, anxious lest one fall foul of the rapacious sharks. The foremost figure rapidly gained the boat and hauled himself up, leaning on the gunwales.

'Good morning, Prince John Bull. May I help you aboard?'

'Good morning, Reverend Truscot, Ali. Would you be so kind as to take me away from here at the speed of lightning?' He grinned and swung himself aboard in a smooth, glistening motion, then looked down and frowned. There was another bang and a ball sailed over their heads.

'It is lucky that Mr Crosby is a bad shot,' remarked Truscot, drily.

'In fact, he is a very *good* shot, but he does not wear his glasses I think. They took all my clothes.' He seemed more concerned at his loss of clothes than his loss of dignity or the risk of his life.

Ali had already begun to row in his upright, oriental manner and they moved rapidly towards the bank. The Krooboys stood off, treading water and awaiting instructions. Crosby stood on deck with a megaphone as if directing a school water-sports. His oaths, however, were of a most unscholarly nature. They rained down upon Truscot's ears like a downpour on an iron roof and with as little purpose. The Reverend stood, doffed his hat in a courtly bow, folded his arms and firmly turned his back on the trader and his profanity. Finally, the Krooboys were recalled. Prince John Bull heaved a sigh of tired relief and ran his hand over his face.

'It was a trade palaver,' he explained. 'They put me in chains and locked me in a room.'

'Outrageous! Why ever did they do that? Are such things normal in the business life of Akwa? Here, take my coat.'

Prince John Bull attempted to insert his massive shoulders into the narrow garment. 'It was on account of Duke Bosun's trust – his debt to the trader. Last year he took much goods up-river on credit. It was a cargo of mirrors. The upland people like mirrors. I do not know why, they are very ugly. Why should they want to look at their own ugliness rather than each other's? Later, he found that he had been overcharged by Mr Crosby and refused to pay. That palaver has been running too long. Because they think I am his niece (*niece? ah, nephew*) they grabbed me and chained me. But I have nothing to do with it. I never set my hand to that paper. I managed to escape through the window but I think, without you, the Krooboys would have caught me.'

'You had best come to the mission and we shall send a message to your father.' Truscot felt almost personally affronted at such behaviour.

They landed heavily and jumped down into the mud, moving through the undergrowth and up towards the house. Butterflies danced in the steamy sunlight. Somewhere a bird sang. Everywhere the blue crabs scuttled in search of carrion.

'Although they still bring bodies to the hill, they now keep them well away from the house. It shows a certain decency of feeling.' Truscot pursed his lips and set off up the slope.

'That . . . is good, Reverend.' King Jack, relenting from his first plan, had changed the boundaries of the 'bad bush', restricting it to the wooded area of the promontory. The mission would not be troubled again.

'But the other day, after the twins came, we found a man whose whole lower jaw had been torn out, he being tied to a tree. His suffering must have been terrible. Who could have done such a thing?'

'It is Ekpo. Maybe a punishment for foolish talking of the society's secrets.' The Prince was stung to defend the humanity of his own culture. 'But it is not as bad as you think. Ekpo victims are allowed to die drunk. Akwa men are not without pity.'

Truscot seemed unimpressed by such compassion. 'Who is the head of Ekpo? Is it the King?'

Prince John Bull hesitated. 'I cannot tell you. No, it is not the King. Do not ask me more.' He waggled his jaw, exulting in the continued possession of it. 'It is our fashion. White men do not understand it. It is the law.'

Truscot felt himself gripped by sudden holy rage. His blue eyes glittered dangerously. 'I will have it stopped, Prince. It may be the law, but the law of Man must always follow the Law of God and that is something I am better able to judge than you.'

They arrived at the house. Silent Will produced a military salute. 'Welcome, Reverend!'

'He speaks for you?' Prince John Bull was genuinely surprised. 'We thought he was dumb.'

Mary, looking pale and wan, a damp towel about her head and a handkerchief held to her nose, came to greet her husband, shocked eyes noting Prince John Bull's undress.

'Aye. Some clothes for the Prince, Mary. Maybe a tablecloth would be best. He can wrap it round him like their skirt.'

Truscot shooed them into the house, calling for hot tea. As they waited, the Prince felt his arm tugged by Ali.

'John Bull. That man without the jaw. Was it . . .?'

The Prince nodded, 'Yes, brother Ali. That was the man who invaded the Reverend's yard with the twins. I had forgotten to mark the door and when he passed it with that abomination, he broke Ekpo. I think maybe it is best the Reverend does not know this.'

'I think you are right, Prince John Bull.'

The King did not just send a messenger. He came post-haste in person, pulled by two large slaves in his 'white man's cow box', jostling on reeking plush cushions. That he was attended by a mere two gunbearers, running behind, and a slave bearing his snuff-box showed that he had come just as he was, without formality. It was a mystery where he had found flat land enough and lanes wide enough to exit from his castle, but contrive it he had. He descended to a fanfare of groaning springs and threw his hat to Ali, pausing balefully in contemplation of the markings by the door. Prince John Bull rose, resplendent in a tablecloth bearing the image of Windsor Castle, to greet his sire. A hushed conversation was conducted in furious whispers, eyes flashing, hands waving, as if to exemplify that mythical language of ancient travellers that was so reliant upon gesture and facial expression to convey meaning that it could not be used in the dark.

'King Jack!' Truscot sketched a slight, unwilling bow. Obeisances to foreign monarchs evoked a fear of idolatry of which Her Britannic Majesty was free. King Jack hurried across the room and clasped his hand in a humid, fervent grip.

'Reverend! I thank you for that you save my son.'

'I did, King, what any man would do.' His apparent tranquillity masked a turmoil of emotions that began to settle into clarity only now that the agitating cause was past. To his surprise, principal amongst them was moral outrage that Crosby should so lightly shoot at them.

'What will you do about Crosby?'

King Jack looked puzzled. 'Do?'

'Yes, King. He fired at your son. He disturbed the King's peace.'

'That be fool palaver. Maybe he only fire at shark to *save* my son. Maybe he save his life.'

'But he cast him into chains.'

'Many time I put him in chains myself.' He laughed harshly and waved further discussion away. His breath smelled of squareface. 'Also I whip him. Crosby no whip him. I complain to Consul before, berra good. Consul fine Crosby one puncheon oil. Fine me ten. One time fool. Two time damn fool.' Their taste for pithy sayings was not limited to those from England then. Proverbs seemed to run in the family. 'That why traders choose this time to make palaver. Consul be here with man-of-war. Come. Don't make Sunday face. I happy today.'

'Why are you happy, King Jack?'

'For that my auntie die today. She lady old too much.'

Aghast, 'You are pleased that your aunt has died?'

King Jack pouted. 'Yes. Of course. I only niece for her. If she no die fore me, no one give her proper funeral. Now I bury her fine. When I die, you see big, big palaver. Big man buried under floor of house. I go be buried on my Liverpool sofa. They have to dig up whole damn country to bury me. Where your wife?'

Truscot was disconcerted by the leap. 'Mary? She had a cold, but now seems to have recovered. Unfortunately her rapid recovery has strained her constitution and she has a fever.'

'I send her my ju-ju man.'

'Too kind, King Jack.' Truscot's absent-minded acquiescence was a mark of his distraction. Whatever the King might say, Truscot was determined to trim Mr Crosby's sails. He thought he knew just how to do it. In his head he began to compose a letter.

Outside the house King Jack paused to consider the Ekpo carvings. 'You do this thing, John Bull?'

'Yes, fadder.'

'It is well. I did right thing when I say Reverend can stay. But I no know he build house too big. He already plant garden?'

'Yes, fadder.'

'You tell women be sure they pour boiling water for all his garden. Better white men don't live for land. Better they on hulks. Then they never learn Akwa language, never reach inland markets, never find out prices. On hulks too they die damn quick too much. When they die, our debt die with them.' He spat. 'Better his garden don't grow.' He poked a fat finger at it like a blood sausage. 'You see to it.'

Greatly disturbed by large black ants that advanced across the yard and threatened to invade our house. The servants lent by King Jack were no help at all but simply upped sticks and fled. So should we, had we had any place to fly to, but it was after dark and we were about to go to our rest. I had hoped for aid from the sacred iguanas that strut everywhere in unconcerned arrogance but it seems that ants are not to their taste, preferring as they do to feast on the chickens of the poor people. (I have as yet made no progress with learning the names of animals in Akwa. When questioned concerning a particular member of God's creation, the servants' only comment is 'that beef make chop' or 'that beef no good chop'.) For Silent Will, however, they clearly did make chop and he set to eating as many as he could.

The ants swarmed in millions, destroying and laying waste all about them like the Philistine hosts. All animal life fled before them, so that our house was entirely purged of cockroaches and other pests. This was the only benefit they brought us. Their bite is more like a sting in that it is envenomed and often becomes septic. They can strip a goat or child to the bone. Our first thought was to protect the twins. Then we strewed live coals in the insects' path, but this was incautiously done, so that our outside washhouse took fire and we were like to lose the entire establishment. Neighbours, however, hastened to our aid and the whole structure was pulled clear of the house. Local youths took great joy in demolishing it beyond that which was strictly necessary. Many then began to carry out our possessions in the misguided belief that they needed to be saved. Several valuable objects went astray in this process. Mary rose from her sick-bed, but unfortunately trod on live coals after the Hindoo fashion and now, it seems – unlike the Hindoos – will be unable to walk for several days. We sought to expel the ants with brooms, but they rushed up the handle and punished us with their stings. White spirits discouraged their attentions, but with so disagreeable an odour and great danger of fire that we needs must discontinue it.

Finally a native saved us with a homeopathic remedy – though not in homeopathic dose. He strewed the nests of the small, inoffensive tree-ants about the dwelling, plucking them from trees, whither the ants returned once their job was done. They swarmed everywhere, contesting the space with all other forms of life and did expel our visitors.

Here I should mention another denizen of the coast, the white ants or termites. These are immensely destructive of books, food and clothes, issuing at certain seasons from the ground in great winged streams. The natives attract them by a lamp set in a bowl of water. Drawn by the light, they drop their wings, perish and are made into a delicious stew. How like to Man who is ever drawn downward when he might so easily soar to Heaven! Curiously, gilt-edged books are immune to them, so that they seldom harm a Bible, a fact that impresses the superstitious hereabouts.

Scarce had we turned the tide of the ants when King Jack's ju-ju man arrived and, having osculated the entrails of a chicken, determined to bury live dogs up to their heads around the borders of the property that they might attract away the malady, which I could not suffer him to do and sent him packing.

It had been a long night and Reverend Truscot was exhausted. Leaving the servants to pick through the remnants of his household and formulate and retell their own mighty exploits in the battle of the ants, he made his way down towards the water's edge. Here there was peace and tranquillity. Not the peace of an English scene, punctuated by the hoot of owls. Akwans related owls to the nocturnal activities of witches and ruthlessly hunted them down. Here was the splash and slither of unknown, unseen and probably legless things, the oddly mechanical sounds of frogs, the mewl of bats, a nature that resolved itself into the rustle of leaves and the purposeful snap of a twig. Moonlight rained down like fine silver, picking out every ripple in the water and etching the silhouettes of the sailing ships like the leafless branches of trees in an English winter. Truscot looked at it all and found it good. There was a polite cough behind him. He turned and found Ali stooped deferentially.

'What is it, Ali?' He tried to hide his irritation.

'*Tuan* is all right? Not hurt?'

Truscot smiled kindly – a waste of time since it could not be seen in the darkness, but perhaps it coloured his voice. 'No, Ali. I am well. I just needed some peace.'

'*Tuan* is sad?'

Truscot sighed. It was the eternal problem of his English ideas of privacy and self-containment. Ali could not understand *wanting* to be alone. If you had no company, it was because you were being neglected or unloved. In the furiously social East no one could *want* to be alone – ever. Alone a man was as lost and pointless as a single ant.

'There is nothing wrong, Ali. I was just thinking that when the time comes, I should like to be buried here.'

'Here?' Ali looked around as if marking the spot. His voice was edged with triumph. '*Tuan is* sad.'

The school was flourishing. The rude benches were daily packed with eager faces of all ages, bevelled by time or sharp and shining with the beauty of youth. What they lacked in scholastic background they made up with enthusiasm, clapping with joy at being able to read and write their own names. Slates being absent, they traced their first rude orthographies in the sandy floor. They soon learned to follow the words of a hymn bellowed out in sheer pagan enjoyment – Truscot guiding them through with his blackboard pointer – and the settlement rang to 'Rock of Ages' and 'Fight the Good Fight'. Class discipline was at a formative stage. Some wove baskets or spun as they listened. Truscot approved their industry. Others chewed kola nut or munched on roasted yams. They got up and wandered in and out at will. Truscot did not seek to check them. They were as yet too close to nature. Confined, they would have pined like caged birds. Young mothers breast-fed their babies as they learned the wonder of adjectives and nouns. The food stalls before the gate did a roaring trade. Initially, there was a shortage of young ladies of the better sort.

'Woman no need sabby book,' explained King Jack when approached by the Reverend Truscot and begged to use his influence.

'Fool woman become fool wife make fool child,' countered Truscot and his case was won. Pithy proverbs made good cases. The royal princess, Adu, appeared next day, immediately distin-guished by her haughtiness and the slave who carried a red parasol over her head. She sat at the back sighing loudly, painting her flawless mahogany skin with brilliant blue geo-metric designs and pettishly jangling her brass anklets. An unexpected pupil was Silent Will, who crept in at the rear, mouth agape. On one of the random sallies into the class that bolstered discipline Truscot came across his letters carved into the floor with such excellence and grace that he was moved.

'You have learnt to write before?'

'No, Reverend. This be first time but I love to learn and I thank you for you teach me.'

Truscot was startled by tears springing to his eyes. In all his long years in the mission field no one had ever thanked him before.

'Stop fidgeting, Mannie. Your hair is a disgrace and must be trimmed.' The Reverend made faces and pulled his head away like a reluctant schoolboy. Mary secretly loved his little childish ways but had the wisdom not to mention this fact. She seized his head and grimly pulled it back within range of her chomping shears.

They were perched on the veranda of the house – Truscot dumped resentfully on a wooden chair with a towel about his neck. Mary wielded her dressmaking scissors with dash and energy, enjoying this rare power over her husband. Prince John Bull looked on approvingly as the fine, thinning hair, once black but now striped with grey, fell to the ground. Truscot's locks lay in a confused fan at his feet.

He heaved a sigh of ecclesiastical dimensions. 'I suppose you are right, my dear. We must set an example. The control of the body is a mark of the control of the spirit. Our reasons are not those of vanity.'

From the corner of the veranda, Ali nodded his agreement. 'Every man must respect his body, *tuan*.' He began to sweep up the hair, pushing it towards the far end of the veranda. He would dispose of it safely later in the place where he buried his own nail-clippings and other exuviae.

'You must be careful, brother Ali,' volunteered John Bull, somewhat too loudly. 'Akwa men use hair for ju-ju. It is very dangerous. If they catch a man's hair, they make ju-ju to kill him.'

Ali tried hurriedly to drown his voice in the swish of his broom but it was too late. Truscot had heard something.

'Eh? What's that? Ju-ju? Did you say ju-ju?' He started up so that Mary involuntarily stabbed him in the ear. 'Ow!' He leaped to his feet and tore off the towel, brandishing it as an oratorical prop. 'Leave the hair, Ali. Let it lie to show the world we defy ju-ju.'

'But *tuan* . . .'

'The people must see that the love of God is a breastplate against the arrows of iniquity.'

Ali paused tiredly and looked pointedly at Mary. He made a hopeless gesture, executing a Levantine shrug amplified by his broom.

'Mannie.' Mary spoke with quiet emphasis. 'Ju-ju is ju-ju, but this is *mess*. You are being silly.'

They paused, frozen in a tableau, contemplating the pile of hair. Blood flowed stickily from Truscot's ear. There was a sudden whir of wings. A small dowdy bird, the same colour as Mary's dress, descended on the sweepings and picked through the locks with the fastidiousness of a lady in a ribbon shop. Unused to European hair, it seemed baffled by this new nesting material. Only after much sorting did it select a strand and fly off to a nearby tree.

'There!' Truscot was triumphant. In some way he had been vindicated by the bird. The others felt it too without being able to explain why. Truscot's hair had entered into the great cycle of nature, the cosmic plan of things.

But a new terror had entered Ali's heart.

'John Bull,' he whispered. 'Do *vultures* build nests?'

*

78

There was no point in being Pharisaical about it. A missionary had to go amongst the publicans and sinners in order to lead them to the light. Prince John Bull had offered to take Reverend Truscot and Mary to the shrines of the local gods and they had accepted. It was important to know the face of your enemy.

In honour of the occasion John Bull had decked himself in a full-length night-shirt of crimson and bright yellow socks. He regarded Truscot critically. Then passed on to Mary.

'I am sorry, Reverend. Missus cannot go dressed like that.'

'What? Why?' Her dress was, as ever, resolutely chaste and drab, a voluminous thing of brown printed cotton.

'It is not decent.'

'Not decent!' Mary's cheeks glowed with outraged modesty.

'It is the leaves, Missus. Your frock covered with leaf patterns. No be fit. Leaves belong to the goddess of the earth and water. No one can wear a pattern like that to the shrine or she has to take it off and leave it there as an offering. You have to come back naked.'

'The goddess of the earth and water is *not* going to have my only brown cotton dress!'

'Perhaps, my dear, it would be best to change. Would a white dress be all right?'

'White is for the priest alone.'

This was all much more complicated than he had thought.

'Green?' he suggested diffidently.

'Green is fine.'

Mary stomped off to reappear ten minutes later in a rather excessively elegant affair of green tulle.

'Will that do?' she asked with definite emphasis.

'That do fine, Missus.' John Bull beamed.

They set off, picking their way down the path to the town, the tight dress obliging Mary to use her parasol to balance after the fashion of a tightrope walker. Children considered their passage with amusement. Women came out of their huts to watch, hands over their mouths to conceal laughter.

'How rude,' thought Mary.

'How polite to hide their inevitable mirth,' thought Truscot, nodding his hawklike nose.

The goddess's shrine was set to one side of the main square, a relatively nondescript affair of wattle and daub with a rather steeply pitched roof coming down nearly to the ground. A surrounding wall of imported red bricks testified to its wealth. As they approached, the tolling of a bell could be heard. 'That means someone is making an offering,' explained John Bull helpfully.

Truscot sniffed. Incense. The old enemy, Popery?

'Please wait, Reverend. I'll go and talk to the priest first.'

This was fair enough. Truscot despised the works of the Devil, but had to admit the property rights of a householder.

The priest emerged, a raddled-looking old rogue with one gammy leg and a wall eye. John Bull had gravely simplified in calling his robe white. It was seamed and stained with a dozen rich juices. He considered his visitors like a tailor sizing up a client and wiped his nose reflectively on his sleeve. There was a long, deep-throated conversation with the Prince, a deal of shaking of heads and looking into space. Then they began to shout in true Akwa fashion, glaring eyeball to eyeball, waving their fists. 'They are negotiating,' thought Truscot. Then came the stage of calm that denied there had ever been a disagreement. They smiled and embraced each other as brothers. They were moving towards a conclusion. John Bull seized Truscot by the arm and led him away. The priest pointed at him and called, 'You be ju-ju man, all same me.' It was meant kindly.

'There is a problem? Does he want money? Is it my calling? Am I improperly dressed? What then?'

John Bull blushed – a difficult thing for one so dark, but it was unmistakable. 'It is Missus.'

'It is her dress?'

'Well. It is sort of her dress.'

Truscot tired of this evasion. 'John Bull. Tell me.'

'All right. I will not beat about the tree. It is Missus. Akwa women do not wear so many clothes. Everyone can see they are not – what is the word? – on heat. But with white women one cannot see. If she were on heat, it would pollute the earth. The priest would die. It is a small matter. The priest wishes to look for himself. That is all.'

'What is he saying, Mannie?'

'One moment, my dear.' He lacked the language to even discuss such a matter with his wife. Such things went unspoken. They were . . . unsayable. 'I cannot ask her such a thing.'

'Why not? How is it that you do not know? With many wives it is difficult, but with only one surely . . . Shall *I* ask her?' He moved purposefully towards Mary.

'No! John Bull!'

'Mannie, what *is* it?'

'Er . . . Well . . . It seems that ladies are not allowed entry today.'

Mary looked like thunder. 'You mean I have come all this way and changed my frock twice to no purpose?'

'I am afraid you are right, my dear. Perhaps you would wait for us. We will not be long, I promise.' He rushed John Bull inside to avoid further discussion.

Within was a concatenation of folly and absurdity that plumbed the depths of superstitious paganism. In the centre the figurehead of a European vessel, depicting a sailor's lass with flowing locks and bulbous breasts. Before her, a hole in the ground into which offerings of gin were libated. (Thus do men ever shape the habits of their idols after those of humankind.) I would not, of course, make an offering, though John Bull did with every semblance of belief, the guardian ringing his bell to direct the wandering attention of the goddess to her supplicant. Before pouring the gin, he executed a sort of parody of military drill with much stamping and saluting.

The priest vouchsafed that at special festivals feasts of bully beef, ship's biscuit and milky tea are held here – such being the preferred food of the goddess. At such times the congregation sit on the barrels of ship's cannon kept here for that purpose. He told me her name was Mammy Water and that she came to Akwa as a shipwrecked nun in the times of the Portuguese. Nowadays, they hold her to be a fair-faced and pacific goddess who lives beyond the sea and sends both European trade and children. She is also the goddess who protects the private parts of ladies from male insult. Perhaps she should start by striking down her priest.

A foul mulatto child is the servant of the shrine and most foolishly indulged. She would fain have taken my watch, it being against custom to refuse her anything, but John Bull distracted her with the sacrifice of his silk handkerchief.

Further depravity was manifest in the debasement of Popish symbols, i.e., the incense and white robes. The adoption of such by the natives in their cult clearly proves them to be superstitious elements and alien to the spirit of the True Faith. A note on this to the mission gazette.

Horrified to see, amongst other figured cloths and flowered china, a picture of our young Queen torn from the *Illustrated London News*. I demanded the priest yield it up, which he at first refused. Later, seeing that I would knock him down and take it by force, he consented if I promised something else in its stead.

Mary, waiting without, somewhat restored to good humour by the open friendship of the children, who boldly approached her with no semblance of fear. John Bull, however, remarked that they thought her the statue come to life, which he thought funny, though I not.

Returned to the mission, I hung our Queen's picture on the wall with great satisfaction. I considered sending the priest, in acquittal of my promise, one of Mary's fashion plates or a portrait of the French Emperor torn from *Punch's Picture Gallery*, but even the use of a foreigner would still have smacked of idolatry. Therefore sent him Mary's brown dress, which seemed a small price to pay for liberating our Queen from heathen bondage. Mary in ill humour again.

Mary sat on the bed and sulked. Mannie would say it was the brown dress. But it was *not* the brown dress – at least not *just* the brown dress. She hated Akwa with an intensity she had not known since the powerful loathings of her childhood. The heat, the privation of simple pleasures, the absence of other white women – all these were normal to her as mate and helpmeet of the Reverend Truscot. To these she had become inured in Singapore. Yet here matters stood even worse. The local women treated her with condescension or contempt. The normal position of an Akwa woman was to be constrained within the yard of her husband like a tethered cur. To wander about on your own was to advertise yourself as a loose woman. Freedom of the body was a figure for lack of moral constraint. That she could not bear. She knew that she and Mannie must not only preach a healthy and moral life, they must live one as an example to their flock.

The twins were a great comfort. She was thrilled and entranced by the tiny perfection of their bodies. Their gurgles and even their cries were the music of life to her. It seemed at last as if she had a sphere of competence allotted to her that was her exclusive preserve. Yet here, too, old discontents found a ready focus. Her marriage had not been blessed with issue. Mannie had never complained, but it had always been assumed that the fault was hers. Barren men did not exist in the Old Testament. She was a somewhat imperfect apparatus that Mannie had become accustomed to and whose failings he had learned to live with, like the teapot with the chipped spout or the chair with the broken spring, another bland proof of his deep Christianity. The children, then, were not to be the fruit of her own body but the result of a sort of act of public subscription, a charitable donation by others. Even her sexuality was gobbled up by the cannibal Church and assimilated to the collecting plate.

She lay on the rumpled bed, sweat dripping from her like despair, and inwardly raged against Africa.

There was nothing approximating a school uniform, indeed most pupils disdained clothing entirely, fretting against the splintery wood of the seats. It troubled the Reverend Truscot to see them thus bare to the world. The worst thing was their total *unawareness* of their own state of deprivation, that they did not feel the lack of clothing. It seemed to him that he might devise a scheme that combined the incitement to virtue with the reward of consistent attendance, yet avoided the problems of the first few weeks.

At that time, prompted by feelings of sheer altruism, he had donated clothes to the children who appeared in class. They had been delighted at this innovation. There had been minor problems, of course. Several of the boys had insisted on wearing skirts, as being closer to traditional male dress than breeches. The young ladies, on the other hand, rose to the occasion as if they had spent their lives among the couturiers of Paris and London. They picked through the garments in question at enormous length, insisting on trying them all, arguing their finer points back and forth. They commented on the lack of flounces and frills, demanded material to make bright sashes, asked for money to invest in the elaborate coiffures that would be required by such dresses. Finally, they would return at all hours of the day and night, faces agonized with doubt, declaring that they had changed their minds about which frock to choose.

Throughout all this Adu held herself aloof, permitting, however, her servant to rummage with the rest. Declaring all the dresses to be unworthy of her, she stalked out naked as she had come, the light striking off the planes and cupped firmnesses of her glinting and faultless body in a manner that led Truscot to admire the Lord in the wonder of his creation.

The next day none of the students wore the clothing they had been given, considering it far too valuable and exotic for all but a special occasion, a death, a fattening or such like. Moreover, all the other mothers from the town were at the door clamouring to receive payment for the attendance of *their* children, so that finally Ali had to drive them away like ants.

In the stillness of the night, as Reverend Truscot sweated in martyrdom beneath the ghostly mosquito net and Mary raged wordlessly beside him, the answer came. Bookmarks!

Among the goods shipped from England were many hundreds of bookmarks donated by an enthusiastic but anticipatory publisher who detected a lively future market in Truscot's endeavours to spread the light. On one side they bore a religious image – the infant Jesus, St Francis feeding the wild birds, that sort of thing – and on the other a suitable text. As frogs whirred and pinged their strange clockwork cries about him, as his wife seethed with loathing against Akwa, the whole scheme dropped quite suddenly into his mind.

The next day he called his pupils to order and laid out the bookmarks on his desk.

'Children!' he called. An old man looked up, surprised. 'Class!' he amended. 'Gather round and look at these.' They swarmed around the desk and began jostling each other. 'See. Here is St Francis, a good man, who fed the animals when they were hungry.' A somewhat effete figure, cowl thrust back to reveal long blond hair, hands outstretched in a shoulder-shrugging gesture. ('Man sabby chop beefs too much,' muttered someone admiringly. 'See he catch birds with bare hands.') 'This is Moses, who brought the Laws of God to men.' A wind-swept, dreadlocked figure, clutching a staff and staggering beneath the weight of a large tombstone, garments tugged by cosmic wind. ('They kill that man. Make him carry rocks too much till he just die.') 'This is our beloved saviour, Jesus Christ, nailed to the Cross. He died for all of us.' A puzzled silence. 'He died that we all might live. He was killed in this way by the Romans but . . . I think we will have to talk about this again later.' ('Reverend forget the story.')

'I shall give you one of these when you are good.' ('House-points' the Consul would have muttered.) 'The boy who sweeps the classroom will receive one St Francis per week. Those who attend faithfully for two weeks will receive a Moses. After a month, you get a Jesus. Keep these pictures and when the mission supplies arrive, you will be able to redeem one Jesus for a yard of cloth or make other purchases at low prices from our goods. Two Francis's will be worth one Moses; five Moses's, one Jesus. Jesus will be worth one manilla. Now let us turn to our work.'

For the rest of the lesson the pupils were rather distracted, but by the time they took their leave with 'To Be a Pilgrim' they had worked out the conversion rate of Francis's to cowries and Jesus's to brass rods. The Coast had another currency.

Mail on the Coast was a rather *ad hoc* affair. Letters to and fro would be entrusted to any reliable officer aboard an appropriate ship. Owing to the uncertainties of the weather and the regular occurrence of shipwreck, a letter might take between six weeks and as many months from England to Akwa. Many never arrived at all. A recent improvement had been the awarding of a legitimate mail contract, as a politically underhand subsidy to the exploitation of the Coast. A real mail box had been brought and stood – bright red and comforting – outside Nash's store. Europeans would travel miles just to see it. Somehow its very presence lifted their hearts. Its contents would be transferred to a bright red barrel with a Union Jack on top, lest it be dropped on the way to the ship. That, too, had acquired almost talismanic qualities. Nash's alone was the right to open it. But the contents brought the same mix of grief and joy as at home, letters from loved ones and feared employers, new regulations concerning trade, bills.

Mr Crosby had just received an especially galling note from his employer, Laird MacGregor, owner of the trading house. It had come to the owner's notice that the Sabbath was not being observed as he would wish, both as the due of the Deity and as an example to the godless, who could not, surely, be lacking in foreign parts. Laird MacGregor was a particularly staunch man in his judicious observation of divine precept. Christianity was good business. Mr MacGregor's personal observation was that God-fearing ships foundered less frequently than those piloted by the legions of the Devil. Crosby was therefore to cease violations of Holy Law forthwith and to make sure that daily prayers were instituted aboard his hulk. It was suggested, with the deference that made it a command, that he should invite the local missionaries or other godly persons to hold occasional sermons aboard. 'For few men are so old and so grown in wisdom as not to profit from a sermon.'

Crosby cursed roundly. 'That damned God-squadder!' Well, he had no choice concerning the holding of a sermon. As for Sunday trading, there was nothing to stop him sending off his boys on trips to the interior on Saturday afternoon. They could not then be expected to stop paddling and allow themselves to be swept downstream, but would have to continue till the next town – their destination anyway.

The same delivery of mail brought dispatches for the Consul. According to an agreement of the European powers, no more guns were to be sold to natives on the Coast, a clear mark that European military supremacy might be in jeopardy. The Consul was instructed to ensure that any guns held in stock by the traders were returned at once to England. This would get them in a fearful wax! He could hear that posturing ass Nash ranting about government interference in trade, the cost of transporting guns back to England, the inadequacy of the British military presence. He laid down the dispatches and turned fretfully to more pleasurable matters.

Also arrived was something much more interesting, a Cadwallader Beer Cooling Machine, housed in a very large wooden crate emblazoned with warnings: 'Danger!', 'Do not tip' (rather like the signs in the hotels at home), 'Beware: Concentrated sulphuric acid'. The device seemed perfectly simple. It relied on the fact that during concentration sulphuric acid, as it gave out water, took in heat. Concentration could be achieved by subjecting a dilute mixture to reduced pressure in a wax-lined steel vessel. Evacuation of the vessel was ensured by hand pumps or by coupling the device to a steam engine of medium power. A contrivance ensured that the heat taken in was removed from a bottle of beer or other liquor placed in a central container. Thus it would be possible to cool beer in any climate. Scuttlebutt rubbed his hands in anticipation. It should be no great matter to couple the engines of the vessel to his Cadwallader. For a couple of shovelfuls of coal a man could finally still his thirst.

Went today to the market. Myself, Ali and John Bull, Mary being afflicted by prickly heat. Met a lad who was an itinerant smith from the Igbo markets further north. He made a great mystery of his craft, cunningly grinding charcoal very fine and placing it on his anvil before hammering red-hot iron thereon. The result – showers of sparks, pointless pyrotechnics with which he sought to amaze the credulous. I showed him by my face and not moving that he had not impressed me – but mayhap those wearing clothes are less at risk from the sparks than the underclad local people. He had some cunningly wrought local needles, the smallest being about the same size as our largest. I offered him a paper of European manufacture in exchange for one of his and he had been like to accept it until one local trader whispered to him to ask for three of mine for one of his. At this, I broke off all negotiation. A missionary may go to a market but need not necessarily act like a fool.

I was impressed at the tenacity with which negotiations are carried out. Prince John Bull is a natural actor and would make a good living on our London stage. While buying a bundle of yams he gave signs of extreme thespian ability, rolling his eyes in horror, shouting in rage, wheedling submissively, wringing the hearts of all who saw him. Poor Ali was moved to tears and offered to pay for the yams himself, at which Prince John Bull clapped him on the back and gave that childlike laugh that makes him a redeemed creature. I almost begin to feel pity for the European traders.

It was noteworthy that most trading occurs as barter, the swopping of one kind of goods for another. Yet copper bracelets, iron hoe blades, bundles of cloth and packets of salt and tobacco – yea, even bottles of gin – seem to function as media of exchange. The local people examine such 'coinage' most carefully before accepting it and reject many copper bracelets because they find their noise displeasing when struck. Curiously, I saw one old woman who has never favoured my class with her presence buy yams with one of my pictures of Jesus. Have I introduced money-changers into the temple before it is even builded? Yet it is my firm faith that the evil growth of slavery can only be removed root and branch not by attacking its bitter fruit alone, but by showing African rulers that it is more profitable to sell the products of their subjects' industry rather than the subjects themselves. In this way commerce becomes a handmaiden of the Lord.

Meat is sold in a large stinking heap, thick with flies, and the different cuts are not studied. Prince John Bull remarked that a regulation brought in by his father is that all flesh is sold with hair and fur attached so that human flesh can be distinguished from that of the beasts. I commended this to him. I instructed the local people how they could improve their presentation of the meat, but they, in their simplicity, only laughed.

Ali, being a devout Muslim, was concerned about gastronomic falsifications and questioned the Prince further when they were alone. 'Is it true, Prince John Bull, that there are those who would pass off human flesh as animal?' Prince John Bull adjusted his skirt modestly and furrowed his brow.

'No, brother Ali. You have misunderstood. They would seek to pass off animal flesh as human. Human is much more expensive than animal.'

'Have you ever eaten it?' Horror was writ large on his face.

'Of course. When my father made me a man, I joined the warriors' society. As a new warrior you must kill an enemy – one of the northern peoples – and eat his flesh with the other warriors.' His voice sank to a confidential tone. 'When Duke Bosun killed his man, he was afraid to go out raiding and so he bought a slave and killed him. But everybody knew. The people here eat much fish and their flesh is very salty. Children you cannot eat, they are too sweet. Also women in milk. Northern men have good flavour, especially the palms of their hands. But Duke Bosun's man had been here in Akwa too long. He tasted salty like us. Everybody knew and mocked him. If he does not become king after my father, it will be because of that.'

Ali felt his stomach heave as at the suggestion of eating pig.

'But human flesh is bought and sold in the market?'

Prince John Bull smiled reprovingly. 'No, brother Ali, that is rare. Not just anyone may eat it. For pregnant women and children it would be dangerous. Also, many of us may not eat pig, or maybe beef or sometimes goat. It depends on your house. In my house we cannot eat a certain salt fish because of an agreement between a water spirit and my ancestor who was helped across a river by that fish. That is why we must be sure what it is that we are eating. The spirits could become angry. A man's belly would swell and he would die.

'But the northern peoples,' he whistled expressively and leaned forward conspiratorially, 'they eat human people too much. In the markets there they have a slave and people come up and reserve the parts of the body they want to eat, drawing them in chalk on the body of the slave. When all the parts are sold, they kill him and divide his body.' He shook his head in bafflement. 'Such is not the Akwa way. We divide up people fairly, according to merit not just ability to pay. Those people are not civilized.'

Another restless night. Scarce had we gone to our couches when we were torn from sleep, confounded by a mighty shouting and drumming, accompanied by a crashing and banging of muskets like unto Pandemonium itself. People were beating on roofs and doors with sticks and ringing great bells. The traders' ships fired off their cannon, so that dementia was made general. Ali dashed into the house with a cutlass and two armed Hausa soldiers, who had been visiting in his quarters, fearing we were suffering an act of violence. We sent out to inquire from our neighbours the cause of this hullabaloo. It seems that we should have been warned, but our innocence of local usage was overlooked. It is the custom to drive out bad spirits from the town in a biennial purgation. As a preparative, rude representations of animals and devils are constructed of twig and clay and set before the houses. The noise is intended to frighten the Devil, but might be supposed to frighten everything but the Great Deceiver. Dogs and cows were driven mad by the din, racing about the streets in wild panic. At first light all the houses were thoroughly cleansed and the animal images broken up and flung in the river. It is unfortunate that the surrounding towns have been unable to agree on a common day for the elimination of spirits, so that they may be held to leave for a few days only till Bonny or Calabar carry out their own affrighting. Then, it is to be supposed, they return together with new friends to swell the fiendish host. It is easily seen that these people are not Christians of the old stamp or they would have persecuted and warred on each other as we did of old about the correct time of Easter.

It was some time before Reverend Truscot learned what had really happened at the funeral of King Jack's auntie. He had returned to the topic of the Crucifixion in his class.

'Jesus died,' he explained, 'for all the things we did wrong.' There was a lengthy discussion between Prince John Bull and a very dark, powerfully built man.

'He wants to know,' said the Prince, 'when Jesus lived.'

'He lived over eighteen hundred years ago.'

'Then, since he's already dead, how may he die for our sins? He died for other men's sins, but not for ours. You cannot hang a man who's dead already. You cannot pay a fine, *then* go around committing crimes with no one touch you. First you do your crimes. Then you pay the fine.'

The dark man folded his elbows truculently. 'I be good man. I never do no thing so bad I like to die.' He looked offended.

'Time is nothing to God. He is not its slave. He died for all of us, John Bull, for you and for me.'

A woman hesitated, then shrieked. 'But for why God kill him own son? He be mad? You think we be fool people?'

'God did not kill him. He gave himself in the place of us all.'

The woman stuck to her point. 'I no believe it, he kill his own son.'

'Prove it, Reverend. Show her your picture.' Picture? Ah, of course, the engraving in his Bible. An emaciated Christ in miraculously unsoiled loincloth, head thrown back in suffering on the Cross. He stepped forward and held it under the woman's nose. The others crowded round, murmuring.

'You see?' Prince John Bull smiled triumphantly. The woman's mouth gaped open, refuted. She nodded dumbly. Truscot shifted uncomfortably in the knowledge that a print was not evidence of anything but the engraver's skill. Still, the important thing was belief. The eye of faith was blind. It was a rock upon which he could build.

'He die all same Ekpo fashion, tied to tree.'

A sigh of comprehension ran around the school building. So *that* was what he meant with this big, long word, *crucifixion* – Ekpo fashion.

'Aaaah! Jesus slave for God.'

'What do you mean "slave"?' Truscot could not have that. Belief was one thing. This was heresy, a new corruption of the Trinity.

Prince John Bull assumed the role of spokesman. 'If a big man is involved in a heavy palaver with Ekpo and fit to die, he can send someone to die in his place. He gives the life of a slave and he can go free. Then they chop off his head or tear off his jaw till he dies. This is just like your God. He took the life of the slave Jesus in his master's place. *Now* we see.' They all nodded in assent. 'It is like the slaves at a funeral for King's auntie.'

Truscot's ears pricked up. The sound of evil slipping through the bush at a distance. 'What's that? What funeral? Explain, John Bull.'

The Prince sighed and clasped his hands, pausing to think before he embarked on his explanation, like a man who knew he would regret what he was about to start. 'When a big man dies, he must not go to the grave alone. Many, many slaves will be killed by his heir or by Ekpo men if he a member, so his spirit be happy. The same happened when my father's auntie died just now.'

'What? Why? But this is terrible. The suffering of innocents. Indeed I have heard of such things before. Why was I not told? I saw no killing.'

'The killing was done in the plantations outside the town. Slaves here are very bad. When their master ill and fit to die, they run away. Not like in the old days. They come back when the killing is over. We give them a cow-hiding but they do not die, so they are happy. The slaves in the plantation had not heard because auntie died quickly. They were far away, so they had not heard the canon of her death.' (Canon of her death – a poetic term for important news? No. Truscot remembered, they fired a cannon when a chief died.) 'So men could go and kill them before they knew fear.'

'This must be stopped. I must talk with the King, with the Consul. This, John Bull, is wicked.'

The Prince turned his unlined, innocent face toward the Reverend, but it was Silent Will who answered, in the longest speech Truscot had heard him utter. 'It be Akwa fashion, Reverend. No man can knock it off. Our fathers do it before us. Our children go do it after we are gone. We be reasonable man. We no kill just *any* slave. Those who live long for one house be safe. It be new slave only who done chop.'

Hauptmann was happy. He had done good business today at the expense of the English traders. His Hamburg office, more efficient than that of the British, had sent him a copy of the new regulations concerning armaments on the Coast. He had known from the beginning that Daneguns and other smooth-bore weapons were exempted. But his rivals had not known and had been eager to sell him their stock at huge discount before the Hausa troops came round and searched their warehouses. They had thought that *he*, poor simple German, had not yet heard of the new regulation and would all meet to giggle at his stupidity. Well, they would see.

Then he had visited a bemused Humphrey Scuttlebutt with the regulations in his hand. The Consul had emerged hot and fractious from a tangle of brass piping and steel vessels, braces sagging and brow wet, to study the fine print for the first time. 'Yes,' he had grudgingly admitted at length, 'looks like you're correct, Hauptmann. Daneguns are all right. I can see that. Tell the other chaps, will you?' He had handed back the regulations, soiled with greasy thumbprints, and turned back to his chemical plant.

'What does it do?' inquired Hauptmann. He stared at the intestinal convolutions of piping and haemorrhoidal bulges, strained his neck to see the plans lying on the desk.

A wicked grin flashed across the Consul's face.

'Top secret,' he declared in a self-effacing manner, tapping the side of his nose with a spanner. 'Government matter.'

An explosives plant, thought Hauptmann in a moment of searing insight. They were building an explosives plant.

Crosby's hulk held itself a trifle aloof from the others on the river, turning its stern to them and its disdainful nose to the open sea. The price paid for such seclusion was a rather longer boat ride from the town than was strictly necessary. The prize gained was the most precious of all on the Coast. This was the one spot where a breath of wind from the ocean stirred the thick, vegetal musk that hung over the swamps. On favourable days it penetrated as far as the jalousied cabins, stirring the papers that lay around in the counting house. The hulk had retained its central mast as the principal support for the roof. At the very apex of the tin covering a look-out point had been constructed with lantern glasses in all directions. By climbing a long staircase from the downstairs rooms, it was possible to attain a crow's-nest filled with a single raddled cane chair, from which the stars and the high sea were visible but Akwa was obscured by a ventilation shaft. This was Crosby's retreat.

It was here that he sat now, studying the letter of rebuke from Laird MacGregor for the umpteenth time, a large pipe – suitable for an Akwa lady – between his teeth. Paperwork did not last long in the Delta. The ink was already beginning to fuzz and blur from the atmospheric damp. A cockroach or some such had made exploratory nibbles at the edges, producing an unwittingly deckled effect. The sweat from his hands had smudged and stained the corner. Red dust adhered to the blotches. The prim phraseology rankled. He wondered if Truscot could have suggested it himself. There was no knowing how thick those two were. It 'suggested most strongly' that he bethink himself of his Christian duty and institute Sunday services on his hulk. 'For the Lord will clearly take against the designs of the ungodly at least as much as I shall myself.'

It did not, however, totally define who should conduct those services or what form they should take. He tapped the letter with the stem of his pipe, smearing nicotine-stained saliva across the palimpsest on his lap. 'Got you!' he smirked.

Inspection of our fields reveals not one flourishing crop. Even the apple trees are as that fig tree blasted by our Lord – proof, I suppose, that Akwa was not the original site of the Garden of Eden and Adam's fall, though the serpent is not lacking. Such agricultural thoughts prompted by the plan announced in *The Times* by Sir John Stephen, a barrister, for draining the Niger River and converting the acres thus recovered into a model garden for white settlers. I fear they would not last a month. Let us hope the King does not hear of it! If we may not have crops, at least we may have beauty. I have planted some roses about the yard to the amazement of the servants. What is the use, they ask, of flowers that are not good to chop?

My sermon today touching on slavery and its evils. Mary unable to attend, as incommoded by some female weakness, which I naturally am unable to understand. I laid great force upon the duties of the master, how he must treat his slaves with justice and mercy. I felt forced to speak my mind concerning the evil practice of slave murder at the funerals of the great and predicted eternal hell-fire for the guilty. Many listened with approval. Struck by the intelligent attention they paid. I found later they were slaves – though some owning slaves in their turn. I spoke also against drunkenness and was noisily supported by a man at the back, shouts and cheers, waving of the hat and so forth. When he loudly called upon the others to heed my words, I discovered he was stupefied with drink. I had rather he had heckled me.

An early morning content reigned in the house. Prayers and breakfast had laid a layer of peace over the domestic circle, like the Saharan dust on the furniture. School would not begin for a while longer. Ali was bustling about, boiling water, quietly singing a plaintive song from his native village. Truscot looked up from his letter and strained to hear the words. Mary smiled across at him. She was making an effort, performing the duties of a chaste and dutiful spouse. She knew that unless she herself spoke, Truscot would feel no need to make conversation. Ali, however, had translated the words of the song to her before.

'It is a beautiful song of regret about his native village. The chorus sings of flowers and trees. I don't recall his village. *Was* it a beautiful place, Mannie?'

Truscot smiled. 'My dear. It is the sort of song produced by all villages at all times, dealing in the imagined charm of the absent. Such songs are no true measure of anything, issuing alike from veritable islands of paradise and absolute hell-holes.' He frowned. It sounded like a pompous rebuke. He had not meant it to. For a moment he nearly apologized, but, as usual, it was shyness held him back. It was a quality that always prevented him making the obvious but appreciated remark that oiled the gears of friendship and love. He saw Mary's lips set as she bit back on her pain. It was too late now to say anything.

'Would you help me with this letter?' He held it out to her. She hesitated, then took it with a sigh and began to read. It was as if the heat of the climate suddenly dropped upon her for the first time. She loved Mannie dearly but sometimes his earnestness was too much for her to bear. The letter was, of course, to the missionary society, Truscot's reply to the plan to drain the Niger. Akwa, it seemed, was to be converted into a model society. Once rapid Christianization had been achieved, the idle townsmen, who now merely inflated the self-opinion of the wealthy, were to be trained as carpenters. Women would be set to weave. The proper task of Akwa was to supply raw materials for the great industries of the metropole. These productions, being in every way superior to local manufactures, could eliminate them entirely from the globe. Yet there were small local crafts that might with profit be preserved and encouraged to avoid the danger of idle hands. In a few short years an almost oriental industriousness would have taken root and slavery be made obsolete by the benefit to be obtained from productive labour. Workshops were to be founded, training given, villages rebuilt along rational lines.

'It is . . . very ambitious. Do you believe such a thing is possible?'

He looked earnestly at her. 'We must make it possible, my dear. We can cater to the spirit only by taking the body in hand. This will not be achieved tomorrow, but it is now that we must start. We must encourage local crafts and not live in expectation of the steamer to satisfy all our wants.'

She might have known. More self-denial. More yam instead of potato, more local pots instead of proper china. Rebellion rose in her but she merely said, 'Yes, Mannie.'

He stood up purposefully and made ready to leave for school. Children were already pushing their faces up against the windows, smearing the glass and crushing their noses into pigs' snouts, staring in unabashedly. Outside they would be urinating against the whitewashed planks. The calm was over.

'Goodbye, my dear.'

Suddenly Mary had an idea. It would, at a stroke, satisfy Mannie and preserve her own outraged notions of privacy. Curtains! She would go to the market and buy local stuff and sew the curtains herself.

'Ali!'

'Yes, *ibu*.'

'Bring money – I mean shells. We are going to the market.'

He appeared drying his hands on his apron and grinning. Ali always loved shopping. They set off at once, Ali bearing a bag of cowries, she a parasol.

It was always a mystery to Mary that there could be so much bustle in Akwa and so little achieved. Where were all these people going? From the market it seemed that rational commerce could surely play little part in their world. Old ladies would walk miles in order to offer a handful of peppers that would hardly pay for the drink they needed to refresh themselves from the journey. Buyers seemed similarly irrational. She heard one man asking about a pile of metal files, 'What be dis ting?' The vendor shrugged. 'I no sabby.'

They haggled briefly and the man went off with one. What he would use it for, Heaven alone knew.

In one corner she espied the fat women who sold cloth. Great lengths of it were hung up on poles driven into the ground. The women pushed kola nuts into their mouths with great fat fingers and heaved their bulk up on to stools as she approached. She began to study the cloth. Most of it was cheap imported stuff, garish prints from Manchester, the sort of material that would serve as the curtain for a lower class scullery. Most of the local weave was thick, heavy cotton, unsuitable for her purpose, or checked material made of small strips laboriously sewn together like a patchwork quilt. The mammies watched her pick through their wares, chewing as impassively as goats, arms dangling limply alongside their thighs. Ali played with his toes in the sand, evincing the classic symptoms of the male set before cloth. There was just one that seemed possible, a darkish blue fabric with geometric patterns – a little savage perhaps, but then her home might be counted a country cottage not a town mansion. It would please Mannie. She seized it. 'How much?'

The mammy spat languorously and stared back at her. Slowly she held up her hand. 'Five hundred.' Five hundred what? And for how much cloth? Mary had no idea what cloth was worth here.

'Fifty,' she said with great firmness. They all screamed with laughter, slapping their hams and throwing their arms up in the air. The woman rose and snatched the cloth back, looking at her with empty, milky eyes.

'Very well,' said Mary. 'One hundred.' Oh dear. This was not working at all.

'Five hundred.'

Mary felt anger stir in her bosom.

'We shall get nowhere until you learn the basic principle of bargaining. I go up. But you must come down!'

The woman turned her head and spat. 'Four eighty,' she said, as if it were an insult that she was hurling at Mary. She seemed about to hold up fingers, then realized the impossibility of fingering this new price and let her hand fall.

Mary sighed. She looked out over the baking market, the swirls of dust that the Akwans called 'dust devils', the filthy children with snot trails under their noses. This woman had nothing else to do all day, no more profitable or agreeable way of spending her time. If it took three days to agree a price, that would be acceptably swift. Bargaining was not something to be got through as quickly as possible. It was a pleasure and an entertainment in itself.

The woman grinned round at her friends. She would ask two hundred, Mary calculated, to which the counter-offer ought to be a hundred and fifty.

'Four ninety,' said the woman. Her friends screamed with laughter at the unexpected tactic. Mary wanted to run at her and ram the parasol down her silly throat. She stamped her foot. Best change tactics before she really lost her temper.

'How much of this cloth do you have?'

The cloth seller pushed another piece of kola nut in her mouth.

'I got plenty. How many arms you want?'

Mary reflected. An arm must be about a yard. 'Fifteen!' she replied with emphasis. The woman swung round for a horrified discussion with her fellows, then turned back. 'Fifteen? What for you need fifteen arms? No be fit.'

'That', said Mary, 'is none of your concern. Fifteen arms. I give you six thousand.' She beckoned to Ali, who dumped down the sack. The woman's eyes followed the bag, her mouth gaping. Relentlessly, Mary began to count.

That was not the end of it, of course. The old woman protested, begged a further handful of cowries, spoke of destitution and starvation, tried to take back the cloth. Mary emerged, hot, sticky, enraged but triumphant. She stood as tall and straight as a queen as Ali trailed along gasping under the weight of the cloth. She had to admit that it had come as a surprise when the woman had come to measure out the cloth. An 'arm' had not been a yard but a length stretching from the tip of one hand across the body to the tip of the other, a 'fathom'. Yet, the basic truth remained: she had engaged Africa and beaten it.

The sewing took some three days, working only when Truscot was not in the house. It was to be a surprise. By the time she and Ali hung the last curtain, her back was stiff and her eyes sore. Yet it did her heart good to look around and see the fruits of their labours, each window neatly sporting two blue curtains. The effect was of savage Africa tamed to domesticity.

'Ali, we have done well.'

He smiled delightedly. 'Yes, *ibu*. It is well.'

The cosy blue curtains had made it a home.

She had been right. Truscot *was* impressed. He turned around delightedly, examined the material, declared it was good. John Bull was less so, hovering on the doorstep, unwilling to enter.

'What I do not understand, Missus, is why you used this cloth, *Akwa* cloth. You are rich enough to buy Liverpool cloth.'

Mary was ready with her answer. 'Because, John Bull, it is pretty and we wish to encourage the local people.'

'But why *this* cloth? It is only used for wrapping the honoured dead. No Akwan can come here. They would die. Your house become a coffin. Your curtains a shroud.' He put his hat on his head and departed in dread.

Truscot and Mary looked at each other. From the kitchen, they were almost sure, came the sounds of muffled giggles.

Unlike most of the trading hulks, Crosby's vessel had a permanent metal staircase affixed to its side. Ali moored his boat and held it steady, passing the Reverend across the front of himself and on to the safety of the stairs. A squall of rain hissed across the water towards them and Truscot laboured quickly up the side to get under cover. Truscot had been surprised to be invited by Crosby to a short (impertinence of the man!) service for the traders. Other boats hurried across the water towards them, bearing white figures dressed in blazers and boaters as if for a Sunday excursion on the Thames – which, thought Truscot, was perhaps only correct. Himself, he wore ecclesiastical black, dulled in some parts and shined in others by a hundred mishaps. In his dumpy black bag, looking suspiciously like a doctor's, he carried the tools of his trade.

Undeterred by the ju-ju curtains, he had fixed upon another local craft to patronize. Hats. It was clear from the amount of imported headgear that a ready market existed in Akwa. The skills of the basket weaver could be easily adapted to those of the hatter as readily as swords beaten into ploughshares. On his head he sported one of their prototypes, a sort of grass bowler based upon the hemispherical baskets of traditional ware. It was still an experimental model. The crown seemed incapable of sustaining its own weight. It lent him a literally crestfallen appearance.

Crosby was at the top of the stairs, eyes gleaming behind thick glasses and wafting vinous bad breath down the stairwell.

'How good of you to come, Reverend. I fear we are making an already busy day yet heavier for you.'

'The cross of service carries itself, Mr Crosby. Where do I . . .?' He eyebrowed an interrogation.

'Oh, through that door, Reverend. Make yourself at ease. Take off your . . . er, hat. About another five minutes and then we can kick off.'

Truscot opened the door into a large room, stepping over a raised nautical sill and plunged into a cloud of cheroot and pipe smoke that made his eyes temporarily swim with rainbows of water. European figures loomed out of the haze. All had glasses in their hands. Nash offered a snarl of leonine greeting. The Consul was on a *chaise-longue* at the far end of the room, speaking with animation.

'Frightfully lucky, really. You see, the servant put the concentrated acid and the water in the wrong containers, so when they were mixed 'Poof' Lost most of one arm, of course, and the beer was ruined, but, do you know, as I stitched him up meself not one murmur of pain. He just sat there and looked at me. Pretty damned unnerving, I can tell you. Had a horse once just the same.'

The King and Prince John Bull came through the door and looked about, bemused. They were ignored, until a servant hurried forward to push a chair into place. Prince John Bull sank, as in a maidenly swoon, at his sire's feet. He was not, it seemed, permitted to sit in his father's presence.

'Welcome, King. John Bull.'

The Prince nodded good-naturedly. A large servant entered bearing the ornate chair Truscot had seen before on the deck of the *Ethiope* and placed it behind the King, who grunted and dumped his bulk from one to the other with the insouciance of a stevedore. The servant took up his position holding the silver snuff-box. It occurred to Truscot that he had never actually seen King Jack take any of the snuff and wondered if the box were empty.

'Let us hope, John Bull, they do not put you in chains again today. It is good of you to come to my . . .'

His words were cut off by a harmonium bursting into wheezy music. Two lines of a popular music-hall song about a man who could eat only fish puffed asthmatically over the chatter.

'*The cats they all love me. They seek out my comp'ny,*' warbled a man in a tight suit. Abruptly, the music died and was replaced by a dour anthem, but the man sang on oblivious, elbows pumping out a plebeian hymn of beery enjoyment. '*The girls, they all flatter me. They pinch me and batter me.*' He was shushed into silence before he attempted further remarks concerning shrimp and cod.

Truscot moved to the front, where a cloth-covered trestle

table had been set up, and put down his bag. He had seen worse than this in the missions in Glasgow, but he had developed an eye for the opportune moment. It was time to begin, before drink got the better of the company and they were beyond the point where a good sermon might strike home. He puffed as he bent down to dig out Bible and prayer book.

'Dearly beloved. Brothers aaaand sisters!' Truscot leapt with shock and looked up. A black man with a wrap-around smile and eyes bulging like organ stops was gesticulating up to Heaven or, more precisely, the roof beams. He had assumed a position behind the table. Truscot frowned at his tight Western clothes, elaborate waistcoat, yellow shoes. He did not greatly care for this – being introduced by a barker like a Newgate pugilist about to go ten rounds. It was – unseemly.

Suddenly the African stiffened as if shot and flung wide his arms in a gesture of crucifixion. 'I thank you for asking me to hold this service. This day is the Lord's. My mouth is the Lord's. This is the Lord's work. Halleluya!' A titter ran round the congregation. A gracious hand, black with pink palm and fingertips, a heavy encrustation around the thumbs as though of nicotine, was extended towards Truscot.

'I am glad to welcome my brother in the cloth here to dine with us at the Lord's table on the Lord's day.'

'Look,' said Truscot, 'what's going on? Does he mean communion? This is blasphemy. What church are you from? Are you even ordained?'

'Pipe down!' This from Crosby. 'Serious matter, disrupting Divine Service.' A murmur of assent welled up from the back like blood in a wound. 'Must be drunk!' someone shouted, giggling.

'According to some, the black man is the unredeemed son of Ham. Yet did our Lord not harrow Hell and redeem all those old sinners way back? The son of Ham is thus redeemed too and enters into his birthright . . .' What accent was it? Jamaican with a touch of American South? A freed slave then, one of those sent back to spread light in the dark continent. He seemed to have absorbed all the worst of Western culture, while losing the best of his own.

'That's not strictly correct – theologically speaking.' Truscot was surprised to hear a shameful quaver in his own voice.

'. . . That is how I am authorized to offer you the Lord's repast.' He spread a sort of soggy sponge cake out on the table.

'What is this? This isn't the Eucharist.' Truscot stared down at it in horror.

Crosby's voice rasped out. 'You've been warned, Reverend. It's not right of you to refuse to listen to a man just because he's African. Very nasty. Very unchristian, I call it.' The traders growled assent and moved forward in the collective valour of a pack of curs.

The preacher raised his voice in sugar-frosted emotion. 'Manna! Manna from Heaven.' He looked down at Truscot. 'From God's castle,' he explained. 'The Lord called upon us to renounce the eating of flesh. Communion? I do not say that my brother in the cloth is wicked, but he is certainly in error when he urges us to a cannibal feast on the living body of Christ. Missionaries have done wrong to introduce cannibalism to the black man. They have set his feet on the downward path.' The traders stamped and hooted. Many had retained their own vessels of secular communion.

'Christ showed us the bread and the wine. "My body! My blood!" he said.' Truscot hated the wobble and gasp he heard in his own voice, the beads of sweat on his forehead.

'Just so, Reverend.' The black man spoke as if to a dim pupil. 'If a man have ears to hear, let him hear. What he willed us to understand was that his flesh was composed of bread, his sweet blood of vegetable liquor only. He was telling us to forswear the flesh of beasts, the swarming progeny of his holy word. But you,' he screamed, pointing at Truscot, 'have perverted his holy teaching to drive us into the arms of Satan by the feasting on human flesh.' Hoots and guffaws, a rhythmic clapping. 'The white man and the black, the white sheep and the black.' His voice was rising again, the Adam's apple pumping up and down. 'Which sheep do you think is the dearer to God?' (Cries of 'Tell us then!') A sudden hush. 'The black, for that he was lost and now is found.' He gripped himself by the hair as if in a fit. 'The black, for that he produces wool.' He seemed to explode in a huge all-consuming shriek of laughter. 'Which is closer to the men of the Bible? The black! For that he circumcises. He makes burnt offerings to his god. White men do not cut their members. White men make no offerings.' He flung up his arms as if to take flight. 'Halleluya!'

'Dear God. Satan!' The heat, the smoke. Truscot felt the deck tip and rush upwards, then settle beneath him. He staggered forward and seized the laughing preacher by the lapels.

'Blasphemy! Blasphemy!' Strong arms pulled him off. His ears buzzed.

'. . . a matter of the greatest possible concern.' The voice was Crosby's, the tone one more of sorrow than of anger. 'Clearly Reverend Truscot is unwell. The climate. The strain. We've all seen it happen before. No shame in it. Immediate repatriation is the only sure solution. You sir, as the Consul, are in charge of the British community. We can't have missionaries importing their own sectarian quarrels. It's bad for the natives, bad for trade. Then, there is worse. There is the matter of the slave labour used at the mission.'

'Slaves?' Truscot gasped groggily. 'We keep no slaves.'

'It pains me to call you a liar, Reverend.' The more-sorrow-than-anger voice was back again. 'But facts are facts and have to be faced. Those two servants of yours. Correct me if I am wrong, but they are slaves.'

'But I knew nothing of this. I hire them from King Jack.' He looked about wildly. 'King Jack. *Are* they slaves?'

The King nodded impassively. 'They be slave right enough.'

'But they are not *my* slaves. I pay them their hire.'

'That's fair enough.' The Consul nodded like a man doing an impersonation of a dotard.

'Not so fast,' said Crosby. 'It's all part of the "free immigration" scheme that the government have just declared illegal in London. It's a scandalous and immoral way for British subjects to get around the fact that under English law it is now illegal to take part in the slave trade. Like Reverend Truscot, the purveyors of this evil do not buy the slaves. They merely hire them. Reverend Truscot is guilty by the same act. If the natives are ever to understand the impartial rule of law, we cannot have one justice for the Church and another for the free trader.'

He held forth a copy of *The Times*. The headline on the back page read, 'Free Immigration scheme is held to be illegal. Participants are liable to prosecution.' He looked at Truscot. 'One of the many advantages of a regular mail service,' he sneered.

'Let me see! But this is good news. *I* wrote to the Secretary of State concerning this!'

The Consul nodded. 'It seems to me that these are serious charges that must be investigated with reflection. We look to the Church to set an example in such matters, to follow not merely the letter but the spirit of the law. I summon the Court of Equity to convene on Tuesday of next week to investigate. All interested parties to appear at that time.' He rapped on the arm of his chair with his signet ring. 'Palaver set!'

BOOK TWO

By the standards of Akwa, King Jack was doing all right. Although Duke Bosun termed him 'brother', the relationship was much more complex. He had come to the town some fifty years before as a very small, very frightened slave, cowering in the midst of a tropical rainstorm. He had been thin and shivering, obviously the runt of that particular slave litter, brought along as not worth deliberate abandonment but uncared for and unfed. By the time he was inside the palisade of the town he neither knew nor cared where he was, having passed through at least half a dozen pairs of hands from the moment of his capture by inland enemies to his arrival on the Coast. He had walked from savannah to forest and now to swamp. The dirt on his feet had changed from yellow to red and now to black, as the language that rang in his ears had changed from polytonal pagan tongues, via terse Arab-influenced languages, to the gargle and heave of Akwan. Beyond here, he was told, lay the blue water and the lands where lived Mammy Wata, the white goddess and her people. His had been a world of immutable certainty, where you were born, lived and died within sight of the same mountain, where dwelt the gods and ancestors who controlled every known thing, the rain, the crops, the cycle by which women's bellies swelled or their blood flowed. That world had been smashed by a single raiding party of armed Fulani, who had joyfully ridden into the village, happily burned it and driven away the people with whoops expressive of simple delight. In his long life he would never be really surprised by anything ever again and lived in constant expectation of discovering that the solid world around him was all delusion and mirror image. When he saw the first sailing ships, indeed the first iron ships, belching fire and smoke, churning the river with their paddle-wheels, he had pursed his lips and passively accepted their existence. When Mr Hauptmann had first demonstrated the effect of the Martini-Henry repeating rifles on a roost of his slaves' chickens, he had not run in fear, but calmly nodded and asked the price. Perhaps it was this quality that had enabled him to accept his lot as a slave; indeed, to turn it to his advantage. He knew now that slavery was the best thing that had ever happened to him, rescuing him from a life of rural idiocy and plunging him into the heady milieu of trade and the sophistication of wealth.

On arrival the slaves had been apportioned to various window-less barracoons around the beaches to await a ship and passage to the Indies. It was considered inadvisable to keep slaves of similar origin together, so they were split up as much as possible and chained at night. The food was sadly inadequate, a few yams, a little water that they contested with the imperious iguanas. King Jack came of an inland race, unused to and disdainful of yams. Many just sat and died, seemingly of despair. Being beneath contempt, he was allowed to wander about the town and so was free to scavenge with the pigs and chickens. But during hours of darkness he must be sure to return. If not, the warriors' society would capture and eat him. It was part of the duties and privileges of the warriors' group – the young men who had not achieved families and trade – to roam the town at night and challenge one and all in the Akwa tongue. In a memorable solar eclipse they had asserted their rights with unexpected vehemence and enjoyed a windfall of surprised victims. Anyone who could not reply in due form was slain and devoured. It was a powerful stimulus to the learning of the language amongst the slaves, and contained and directed the destructive tendencies of the young into channels that brought public benefit. But occasionally, like the boastful and short-lived adulterers of the slave quarters, King Jack would brave the dangers of the night, dodging the silent groups of dark men, clanking with metal and exuding the fierce musky smell of Akwa males, to devote himself to an even more dangerous pursuit.

His gleanings from the rubbish tips were inadequate. His wide, helpless, hungry child's eyes were too common a sight in Akwa to touch the hearts of the more solid citizens. He had learned to fend for himself. He ate iguanas. They were large and incautious, having a softer life by far than the slaves, seizing and consuming all with impunity. As the messengers of the gods, no man would dare lift a hand against them on pain of excruciating death. Even to injure one by carelessness or accident was held an offence against the earth. They belonged to no one. No one had counted their numbers. They would not be missed. At night, in the sleazy habitations on the edge of the town, he would hear the thud of their tails and the bandy waddle of their feet as they stalked about the streets with the same arrogance as the warriors. He was careful to take only the smaller ones that he could kill with ease and consume entirely, roasting their flesh in a fire down by the water's edge. The bones he flung into the water. No one had ever caught him. No one would ever know. He began to fill out and grow.

It seemed to him only just that as the warriors ate the slaves, the slaves should feast on the fleshy embodiment of the warriors' god. By the simple act of the culinary domination of iguanas he felt himself to make the city his own and in his heart became its ruler. The city seemed to have accepted the secret covenant, for it sent him good fortune.

Most of his fellow captives languished, waiting for a Spanish slaver that was repeatedly delayed. The middleman grudged them food, seeming to want to take out on them his financial insecurities. King Jack, however, underwent spectacular elevation. He was assigned to old King Robert's household. A first son had been born to one of his many wives. It was the custom to assign an older slave child to each gentleman's son as companion and protector. A simple ceremony made it a bond of blood that lasted to the grave and beyond. Jack was quite simply the only new slave who was not ailing and pining. One morning he was terrified to be seized by a group of warriors in the yard and interrogated in Akwan. It was fortunate that he had picked up the rudiments of the tongue, though he spoke a female form gleaned with his scraps in the kitchen, rather than a male form. Male and female had different words for the most everyday things. They laughed at him, but their amusement protected him like a talisman. He was spared the knife and led to the iron-sheeted chiefs' house and presented to the ancestral altars. His head was shaved, he was circumcised, fed and told that from now on his name was Jack. His old name he had now forgotten.

He and the present Duke Bosun, the old king's son, had risen together. Like many slaves, his loyalties were not subject to the tug of conflicting forces. He sank or swam with King Robert. As a child, when Bosun had committed some offence, it was Jack who was punished in his stead, a whipping-boy, as no gentleman would suffer chastisement except at his father's hand. Apart from King Robert, no one else would help or protect him. His fidelity was absolute.

By astute trading he had accumulated a sufficient competence and had been allowed to set up his own trading house and build his own war canoe. Under the wing of royal preferment, wealth had quickly followed. With wealth had come rivalry, the folly of ostentation. Jack had unwisely invited King Robert to visit him in his new house. In welcome, he had laid a path of copper rods from the creekside landing place to his door so that the monarch would be spared the need to sully his feet. King Robert had arrived with feet unsoiled but mind troubled. A man as rich as Jack had become could be a dangerous rival. Evidence of the withdrawal of royal favour swiftly followed. A series of disputes about markets culminated in two of his slaves being sent home with their hands nailed to the bottom of their canoe and their noses slit.

Jack bided his time and suffered with equanimity. But he was not inactive. In the plantations and settlements there sprang up a new group – the bloodmen. They took a covenant of mutual aid sealed in blood. Most horrendous to Akwa ears, the blood was not human blood but that of the iguana. The bloodmen made their first and most dramatic appearance at old King Robert's funeral. The warriors who descended to the plantations for the ritual killing were surprised to find the gates shut against them. Worse, those inside were armed with Daneguns and schooled in their use, refusing to yield so that they could be slaughtered to keep Akwa traditions. No one had ever done this before and the warriors were baffled. Duke Bosun and the old nobility railed and ranted, but to no purpose. Apart from a few miserable household domestics, the old king's death was unmarked by great slaughter.

A crisis rocked the town. Two factions formed and stared at each other across a divide of blank enmity. Jack alone spanned that divide with urgent diplomacy. Through his status as both househead and slave he was able to negotiate a return to loyal service against guarantees of abolition of the slaying of established slaves. New purchases would still be subject to immolation, but that was regarded as only reasonable by all parties. They were, after all, not members of houses. Old slaves were eager not to gain their freedom, which would have meant an end to protection. They had seen how free men hired by the day were treated by the white men. When not needed, they were cast off to starve, whereas an established slave could not be denied his food even if his master had to sell his wives to find it. In the old days the worst form of punishment had been for a man to disown his slave. Such wretched creatures had no means of sustenance or source of protection and could be killed with impunity.

A new power had come to Akwa and its recognition was the proclamation of the reign of Good King Jack. To celebrate, he had a dozen slaves killed – all new imports. The gesture effectively silenced Duke Bosun, for the moment.

It was raining when the French naval sloop *Héloïse* dropped anchor in the bay. Two officers were on deck fussing with their uniforms and luggage. Captain Rainier, a tall man who somehow contrived to look dapper – a quality normally the exclusive property of the short – scanned with distaste the harbour sheds and muddy beaches. There came the firing off of a gun and acts of irrelevant nautical precision with signals before they embarked, rowed by four spotless matelots under the flag of France, for a meeting with the chiefs' council.

In the fluid conditions of the Coast, with contesting local petty monarchs, foreign powers felt it essential to make as many bilateral treaties as possible for the protection of trade. There were no French nationals in Akwa. It is true there was Monsieur Dufief, a man of somewhat *louche* appearance, who ran a house of pleasure staffed by mulatto girls and claimed French nationality as his own. There was, however, no documentary evidence of such a link and, anyway, he was of such dark complexion as to cast doubt on any such pretension. Nevertheless, before England declared a definite colony that included Akwa, the French were eager to collect as many signatures and crosses on as many vaguely-worded treaties as possible, giving grounds for possible intervention at a later date, a potentially valuable stock of future grievances.

King Jack had made no bones about his own position. 'I be Englishman,' he had declared in his own *civis Romanus* style. The declaration, however, was double-edged. While the Consul understood this as a mark of Jack's submission to his own authority, Jack took it as indicating his full equality with any other man, be he white or black. When the French had announced their visit, Jack had deemed it politic to be absent and had withdrawn hastily to his plantation. Where the French were concerned, either a 'yes' or a 'no' could be equally a source of trouble. The French, then, were greeted at the castle with shrugs of almost Gallic exaggeration and expressions of empty regret that they found particularly galling. Yet a meeting of the chiefs had been called by one named Duke Bosun, perhaps they would be so kind as to attend?

The meeting was held in a long, narrow house roofed with brass pans – 'Neptunes' – beaten flat, the floor studded erratically with quarry tiles. The Frenchmen regarded them with distaste as signs of English influence. Worse was to follow: gin served into cracked beakers from a brass spittoon. The Akwans watched carefully as the Frenchmen swallowed and mimed ecstatic enjoyment. The glasses were ruthlessly refilled. Duke Bosun observed their shuddering distaste. Would they perhaps prefer English tea? They declined.

The French were in dress uniforms, tricorn hats and swords,

the Akwa contingent in even more resplendent finery, the debris of two hundred years' association with the British navy. Duke Bosun sported an admiral's plumed hat encrusted with gold braid plundered from other uniforms, now no more, and had sewn epaulettes on his long gingham shirt. In his hand he held a brass telescope and on his wrists were ivory 'trust bracelets' given by European traders and inscribed with declarations of his probity. Many of the others wore top hats and carried canes and swords. One had elastic-sided boots and one of the new police helmets rammed down on his gaunt features.

Where was the King?

The King was regrettably detained, but that was of no matter. A king here was not as a king in France, all powerful. Here a king ruled in concert with his chiefs.

The chiefs were misinformed. In the recent history of France there had been several kings. They, too, were subject to the popular will. Should they become tyrants, they would be displaced. Captain Rainier looked uncomfortable during this controversial résumé of contemporary French history. His companion raised an eyebrow quizzically. In the navy political orthodoxy was required.

Indeed? Such fashions were good. In Akwa, too, tyranny was not tolerated. It was indeed the case that Akwa men and Frenchmen should be brothers. Both sides bowed.

'Good-day to you!'

This cordial understanding was brusquely dispelled by the entry of a black-clad Englishman in a curious hat with sagging crown.

'Excuse my interruption, gentlemen. I understood the King was here.'

The King was not here, Reverend. See, there were only these gentlemen of France.

'French, eh?' To the chiefs' dismay, he sat down with a

purposeful look upon his face, his weight pitched forward on his stick, scanning their faces. There was a silence. Captain Rainier cleared his throat.

He had come to bring fraternal greetings to the King. In his absence, perhaps he might offer these few unworthy presents to the chiefs. A deprecating gesture. He stooped and unbuckled the lid of a trunk, flinging it open to reveal a mass of gimcrack trade stuff. The chiefs leaned forward to peer in. Captain Rainier plucked forth an exemplar and held it aloft with simple pride.

Regard the wonder of this object. He made a swift adjustment underneath and set it down, settling back, smiling, to observe its effect. There was a harsh skirl of cheap metal and a stir ran round the chiefs.

Only then did Truscot realize the true nature of the thing. It was a clockwork elephant, no less. Setting off apace, tin-plate bodywork gleaming, its insides gnashed and whirred with metal teeth. Felt ears flapped mechanically. Gathering speed, it thudded into the legs of Duke Bosun, who let out a squeal of outraged modesty and fell off his chair, skirt flapping. 'Debbil ting!' From there, it swerved with deflected but unabated zeal, smashed into the gin, sending glasses flying, and set off grimly for Reverend Truscot. He pitched forward and raised his stick, inverted as in a parody golfing stroke. With one blow the irksome beast was toppled on the quarry tiles and lay, legs scrabbling like those of a felled cockroach. It whined and emitted a sort of metallic belch, then, rasping, ground to a halt. Truscot picked it up with his fingertips as if fearing it might come back to life. 'Not, I think, best Birmingham,' he remarked to chiefly laughter.

Rainier flushed and pulled forth a sheaf of documents penned on very thick paper. Already the ink was blurring in the damp air. To more serious matters. There was the small business of a treaty, a written declaration of amity, a formality, of course, but it would allow the captain to disburse further payments. See! A small signature, or even mark, just here was all that was required.

'I strongly advise against the signing of any such treaty without the presence of the Consul.' Truscot leaned forward to take the papers. 'What is the precise nature of this document?'

Zut! This was perhaps not a matter that regarded *Monsieur*, a private matter of diplomacy, a mere formality, a trifle between friendly peoples. Still, perhaps it was best left for the King. Hastily, Rainier stuffed the papers away. All the chiefs were invited aboard his ship for refreshments the following morning. Alas, it was likely that *Monsieur* would be prevented by other business on a Sunday. A small smile played about Rainier's lips. In the meanwhile, perhaps Duke Bosun would extend an old French civility and agree to fly this mere unworthy example of a French flag on his boat for the visit. Note how pretty were the bright colours. He extended a warm hand to the chiefs, a glacial salute to Truscot and exited whispering emphatically to his aide.

'Beware, Duke Bosun. They mean to ensnare you and take the country. Do not set your hand to any paper and do not fly that flag.'

Duke Bosun smiled. In common with most Akwa men of his generation his two incisors had been knocked out, transforming his dentition into a sort of hyphen between two black dots. It contrasted oddly with his single, unbroken line of eyebrow.

'I sabby that flag big ju-ju for white man. Flag be fetish strong too much. He think, you put flag for one place, he king of that place. I give it to one of the women.' He shook his head at such folly, then shot a suddenly sharp look. 'Englishman no try take country?'

'No, Duke Bosun! The white Queen of Liverpool has treaties

with you and will protect you even against her own subjects.'
He pushed an unworthy doubt to the back of his mind as one
would swat away a fly. After all, the Queen's representative, the
Consul, might not be an intellectual or moral giant, but he *had*,
in the long run, dismissed the charges against Truscot – though
with an impertinent hortation to greater prudence in worldly
affairs. To mention her own exalted personage in the same
breath as the suggestion of deceit and perfidy brought sweat to
his brow.

Duke Bosun plucked fretfully at his skirt and hitched it up to
reveal a stick apparently bound to his thigh with string. He
pointed a stubby finger at it.

'I think all Liverpool man treat black man all same this fella.'

'I'm sorry, Duke Bosun. What is that? A charm? Some ju-
ju?'

'That be guinea worm. He live for body. He hurt you too
much. All your body hot and sick. One day he poke out head.
You catch 'im quick and tie head for stick. Every day you pull
out little more, one day, one inch and tie for stick. You pull out
too much, head come off. But guinea worm just duck back
inside and grow new head. Us Akwa men be all same that
worm. White man wind us in little bit each day. Careful they
no pull too much. They pull too much, maybe we lose old head
– old king – but we grow new king for sure.' He flashed a
knowing look at the other chiefs, who replied with gap-toothed
smiles and nods.

Truscot savoured this earthy style of sermon. There was
seldom a man so versed in scripture and so wise as not to
benefit from a sermon, even one fixed upon a heathen faith.
The elephant emitted a final expiring clank and fell silent. The
damp of Akwa was already gnawing at its vital parts.

Truscot declined their offer of gin and took his leave, doffing
his hat in salute.

Duke Bosun stared after him wonderingly. 'For what,' he asked, 'that man wear basket on head?'

Returned late from Duke Bosun's house. Mary still abed with *croucrou*, an affliction that makes her skin flake off in painful patches. The twins, mercifully, asleep. Scarce had I robed myself for bed when there came a rapping at the door. It was a poor unfortunate woman whose husband had just died. I had visited him on an errand of mercy the night before, but his death warrant was written in his face and I could but give laudanum to ease his end. I sought to comfort the lady in her loss and fell to my knees to guide her into the gentle paths of prayer, but this was not the comfort she sought. I had, she declared, killed her husband with my remedy and must now agree to replace him in the duties of matrimony. Her impertinence did not end here. The deceased, being a man of generous sexuality, was possessed of seven wives and it seemed I was to serve them all. They had, moreover, all accompanied her and set up a fearful banshee wailing from the gate, thus waking the twins, who began to cry. I called Ali, who drove them away with firm but gentle strokes of his broom.

The following morning Prince John Bull was in the yard, calling in on the way to the market. His elegant clothes were spattered with a mixture of black and red mud, his good straight features glistening with pearls of perspiration. He regarded his ruined appearance with pain. In his hand he held, rather sheepishly, one of the Akwan hats promoted by Reverend Truscot. That he should so compromise his dress showed evidence of a true friendship that touched Ali's heart. He took him straight to the kitchen and allowed him to wash, then dosed him with hot sweet tea. From a metal pot he ladled a helping of spicy curried fish.

'Ah! That is better, my brother. I have come far, from the plantations.'

'King Jack is still at his farm?'

'King Jack is . . . unwell. He feels himself threatened. There are many signs. He caught one of his wives going to a ju-ju woman for medicine. She claims, of course, it was to keep his love to her. They always say that. But he sabby it was to kill him. What is this fish?'

'I think I should not tell you. Maybe it is forbidden to you to eat this fish. What will happen to her?'

'That is well. Where there is no knowledge of crime, no law has been broken. She will be killed. To attack the King is to threaten a big Ekpo man. So maybe he will have Ekpo kill her. Maybe he will do it himself.'

'Is this why you have come to town?'

Prince John Bull stretched out his legs and sighed with the delicious anticipation of a tired man who sees a soft bed before him. 'I have come to buy saucy nut.'

Ali frowned, darkly. 'What is that? Is it for cooking?'

John Bull laughed a good hearty laugh and cracked his fingers, turning his hands outwards and pulling them both against each other. 'Brother Ali. Always you think of food. No. It is for the poison ordeal. If a man drinks the water of the nut and vomits, he is innocent of crime. If he does not vomit,' he yawned ecstatically, 'he will surely die of poison and was guilty. But usually I don't even need to take nut back. For me to ask the price of saucy nut in the market is enough to scare the women to stop their wicked ways. They turn into a new leaf. But now I must go. I shall sleep like a dog.' He rose and clapped the damp hat on his head, stepping out into the sunshine and sniffing the air like a pointer. 'Soon the smokes will begin – the dry winds from the north that bring down red dust. That is when the white men go mad. Thank you, my friend. We will meet again soon. How is the Reverend?'

'He still sleeps. He was up till late replanting the fields. It seems as if nothing will grow in this place.'

'And the Missus?'

'As always, she is sometimes sad. And her body has scabs.'

'That is well. It is perhaps from the elevation.' He looked out across the bay. 'The French ship is still here, but they will leave as soon as the fever begins among the crew. Ah!' They watched as a long Akwa canoe moved out from dark shadow at the edge of the water and approached the vessel. As it passed into sunlight, there came a sudden blaze of colour from the rear, where fluttered a large French flag to which had been stitched the name 'Duke Bosun'.

'So.' He protruded his lower lip thoughtfully, displaying its surprisingly bright inner pinkness. 'I think I must go to the market with all dispatch. Perhaps it is time my father came back to the town.'

Only today did I hear of the terrible goings-on at the King's plantation. Hearing me speak out often against the ill-treatment of slaves, the 'bloodmen' flock to my sermons. This no doubt offends the old nobility, but the Christian message has always been a message of hope to the poor and downtrodden. One of these it was who broke the dreadful news to me. Dozens of innocent women have been put to the ordeal on some imagined charge. Deluded by the Devil, the King believes his every ailment due to the wicked wiles of the sex, when the evil is less in the hearts of women than in his own excess of squareface gin. I questioned John Bull on the matter. He impudently explained that it was from reform and the influence of white men that the King found himself driven to such dire expedients. In former times the threat of deportation or death at the funerals of the mighty contained the rebellious spirits of the slaves. Now this is no longer possible, so what is to be done with the unruly? I remarked that it seemed to me there were chastisements enough in Akwa without resort to the supreme penalty. I asked concerning his sister, Adu, who has not attended the school for several weeks. It seems that she has been clapped up in the fattening house and will not be set free until deemed sufficiently gross for marriage. Her spouse is a blind old man fifty years her senior with twenty barren wives already. All this augurs ill, for she is a girl of spirit, as I know to my cost.

But Truscot was shortly to see Adu again. Passing through the town, he was struck by the unusual activity centred on the smithies. These were a collection of simple thatched shelters without walls set well clear of the wooden buildings of the main settlement. From within came the sound of fierce hammering and the glow of some great fire. Casting in a curious glance, Truscot was amazed to see a pack of blubbery women from the fattening houses, the fire glistening on their oiled skins as though on the pelts of seals. Even more astonishing, there in the centre was Adu, bloated to a virtually featureless blob, applying herself to the bellows with an energy she never showed for her schoolwork. 'Adu!'

She looked round and grinned sheepishly. His heart ached for the loss of that spare and angular form.

'Adu. What is this? Have you become a blacksmith?'

'No, Reverend. This be for Mammy Wata. All women need new bangle for Mammy Wata, so we got to help.' She pumped away, breasts flopping like puppies' ears, puffing in her new middle-aged corpulence. 'Me, my sister, we come here get bangle fix one time.' Without pausing in her pumping, she held out a wrist around which was twisted a wrought-iron bracelet with flared ends, rather like a deformed stair-rod. In fact, it *was* a stair-rod. It must have been applied when hot and was irremovable. It nestled into the rolls of fat around her limbs.

'And what is your part in these activities, Adu?'

'Oh, Reverend,' she clapped her hands together in a childlike gesture of excitement that moved him. 'I dance! All we women from fattening house, before we marry, dance for Mammy Wata at riverside. You come. You watch. Tomorrow.' Truscot thought how much more becoming to her was this simple excitement than the sour pouting of her schooldays. He *would* come.

To the waterside to see Adu indulge her terpsichorean propensities. John Bull urged the necessity of making an offering to the shrine. This I could not countenance, but allowed him to make a present in my place. Sun very hot. The streets thronged with people in festive mood. The flies a great trial. The Africans permit them to run in and out of the corners of their eyes, drinking up the moisture. Mary suffering from a heat rash that prevents her wearing sufficient clothes to leave her room, where she is thus confined by the dictates of modesty until improvement. Here she sews and studies her Bible.

The festival – for so it turned out to be – was a very jolly affair. The ladies were untroubled by inadequacy of *their* garment – a simple grass skirt – making up for it in the wealth of bangles and charms with which they had adorned themselves. Particularly striking were rude necklaces of rough coral beads, each the size of a rock, worn around their necks. Bystanders told me they were the gems taken from the jewel chest of Mammy Wata following some combat between herself and the Akwa people. The movements were not without a certain brutish elegance, recalling rather the simple revels of country folk in some of the wilder parts of our own country. The whole effect was largely spoiled, however, by their soliciting of gifts, pushing saucers into the faces of bystanders so that they would place offerings of money and kola nut upon them. I gave to none but Adu in token of friendship.

Various masks were in attendance, hideously formed after the faces of animals and fish, carved from wood and painted in the loud hues of idolatry. The entire body of the dancers was covered by a tight costume resembling that of Ekpo runners. They capered and whirled to the accompaniment of wild drumming, which seemed to exercise an invigorating and tonic effect even upon the Akwans.

The high point, however, was a sort of water pageant. A large canoe had been prepared, rowed by men in dress of special leaves and towing behind it a sort of rude raft. The priest of the shrine was aboard and saluted me most civilly. He would have suffered me to ride beside him but this I declined, not wishing to associate myself with dark rites.

On the raft sat the appalling mulatto child, smirking in a fashion that evinced lack of sufficient correction and, what is more, wearing Mary's dress of brown leafed stuff – which would not have pleased her. She was bedecked with all manner of European ornament, earrings, rings worn *over* her gloves, even a pair of spectacles, and cooling herself with a Venetian fan. About her were ranged the goods of Manchester and Birmingham – brassware of all kinds, printed cotton stuffs, squareface, tins of tea – all stacked as if in some mobile grocer's window or, perhaps, rather a tableau of British products at some fair. The simpering creature was towed out into the river to the great pleasure of the public, who hooted and stamped their delight, possibly in anticipation of the dreadful child receiving a good ducking. Many threw flowers and other things in the water. Men emptied bottles of gin into the river but not, I fear, from any excess of teetotal zeal. These were offerings to the goddess. Alas, the spoiled child remained unbesmirched, though immersion might have been a valuable physic to her and, I confess, I hoped for it. She disappeared around the headland unducked and immensely pleased with herself. It is important to see such local customs since such edifices of superstition are to be dismantled to provide the bricks whereof we may build the Church of God. We have here the basis for a fine Christian festival of purity. It is far better to have a people who love the water too much rather than too little – the latter being the normal case with Africa.

Round the headland the river met and united with the sea. Here the Atlantic waves surged against the wall of deep, fresh water that flowed with relentless persistence from the heart of Africa. Here the currents and tides boiled and swirled in deep eddies and troughs. Here it was that they began to pile rocks on to the raft until it sank lower and lower, soaking the brown dress and spoiling the painted Venetian fan. The child still giggled and smirked as the raft dipped beneath the waters with a dull gurgle that passed unnoticed in the roar of the sea.

Ali was way out ahead, cutting recalcitrant creepers with swipes of his machete. Occasionally he cast solicitous glances at Truscot, who stomped goutily behind. The path was well defined, being kept clear by the constant traffic between plantations and town. The trees towered high and were topped with a frizz of palm leaves. Truscot did not know what fruit they yielded if, indeed, they yielded any fruit at all. Had the Garden of Eden been like this? He thought not. Surely here the mosquito had been created together with the serpent, and the cursed mangrove fly must perforce have originated when sin was given licence to run free and further tempt fallen Creation. Birds sang away in the tree-tops, a dark, waving umbrella that made him giddy when he looked up. *Sing* was not the right word either. The birds here did not sing. They squawked and squabbled like Akwa people. One had an odd call consisting of a descending cadence of notes quickening towards the end — rather like a ball bouncing down a flight of stairs. It was cooler in the forest than outside, but the air seemed thicker, almost liquid. The light too had a green, underwater quality and lichen swarmed over trees like seaweed. Everywhere life seethed. The bearers strode at a dogged pace, trunks and bundles on their heads, John Bull's trade goods and Truscot's own supplies. The precise logic of it all escaped him. Half the bearers seemed to be carrying supplies to feed the other half. At the rear was Silent Will, mysteriously bearing nothing at all, but followed by a small boy who carried *his* supplies. At this point Truscot had put an end to the nonsense and refused further attendants. At their feet ants crossed the path in their own long file, leaves waving in upraised jaws as if for some lesser market.

Prince John Bull returned down the column. 'How are you, Reverend? Are you sure you would not prefer to ride in a hammock?'

'No, thank you, John Bull.' He waved his stick, ant-like, above his head. 'As long as I have this, I am well enough on my two feet. How much further?'

The Prince dusted leaf-mould from his sleeve. 'Another two hours should do it and then we shall come to my ramshackle.' Truscot smiled at the word.

There was a whoop and an excited shouting from the front. Men flailed with sticks. Then came the unmistakable sound of Ali shouting in triumph. He appeared, face aglow like a boy's, holding up the body of an eight-foot-long snake as thick as his arm. For a moment Truscot thought it was a python. Pythons were sacred to at least half the Akwa. This would not do. There would come a time for confronting the old beliefs, but that time was not yet. Then he saw John Bull's face catch the flame of delight from Ali's. No python then, just a common serpent in the garden. The bearers claimed it for their own. Later they would stew it and eat it.

They came to a village on the bank of a creek, black mud heaped up all around as if by some giant burrowing animal. The people were cautious at first, circumspect. Strangers had always meant trouble here. They hung around the doorways of their huts, though, flimsy as they were, they offered scant protection. Emboldened, they came out and requested to trade. 'What thing you got? We give good price.'

Truscot found it hard to imagine that they had any goods others could conceivably want. 'I no live for trade,' he panted, 'I be God-palaver man.' They grew insolent then, refused water, bloodmen all. Some of the younger ones shouted jeers and called him a poor thing to come to them empty-handed and bringing no profit. John Bull came back to hurry him on.

'Bad people, Reverend, slaves from a ship that wrecked near here. Best we move on.' Of course, the moral strength of one's position held no guarantee of the nobility of one's thoughts and actions. Slaves could be bad men too. Text for a sermon there.

The jeerers followed to the edge of the forest and left them with gestures whose precise meaning was not clear but manifestly hostile. One railed against the white God-man, staggering with drink, challenging him to strike him with lightning to demonstrate his power. As he passed, John Bull felled the man with a casual swipe of his fist. 'Just so,' thought Truscot with satisfaction. 'Often a man may with impunity insult the high ruler and be undone by insolence to a special constable.'

By the time they reached the King's plantation, or 'ramshackle', pools of darkness were forming in the hollows and gather gathering around the trunks of the trees, extending a tentative finger of blackness towards the palisade and the collection of wattle-and-daub huts. Splinters of fire gleamed through the cracks in the walls. Someone fired off a cannon to announce their coming. A fart of acrid smoke pulsed across the central clearing.

The people gathered together to stare at him and greet John Bull. The Prince was clearly popular. Men and women patted him like a favourite pet. Children (his?) clung to his legs stickily. He was young to marry certainly, but such was Akwa fashion. Marriage was not a matter of personal whim but properly organized, as in the English merchant class, to assure valuable allies in trade. 'Early to bed, early to rise,' as the Prince had pithily put it. A woman pressed a piece of roast yam into his hand. There would be business to attend to, that of a king to his ambassador and that of a father to his son. Truscot settled stiffly down under a tree to wait – like an old dog. Someone rushed up and urged a stool upon him. A woman handed over a calabash of cool water with gestures whose grace belied her massive bulk. He nodded thanks.

As he looked out over the trampled ground he hoped that Mary was better, feeling guilty that he had not thought of her all day. Later he would say a little prayer.

'Payment is a matter of no importance,' said Hauptmann, waving the question aside. It was not a statement that had often been made in that particular dwelling.

They stood in the house of the lone French resident of Akwa. Monsieur Dufief's calling was not a noble one, as was apparent from the position of his house. At the eastern end of the waterfront stood the minor outposts of consular authority, then, moving westward, came the hulks and sheds of the traders. Furthest down river, downwind and down sewage stood Dufief's house, hard by the native quarter. It was a house in more than the architectural sense, for it was here that he kept an assortment of mulatto girls and runaway slaves to cater for the simple and brutish appetites of visiting sailors. The house, too, was mulatto and leprous, painted with blotchy yellow stucco with green patches of sprouting moss that drove roots deep into the exposed areas. Slatted blinds hung sluttishly on sprung hinges over the windows, eked out with filthy curtains. The yard was littered with nautical debris, as though the patrons were wont to wander in with large anchors under their arms only to forget them in the heat of sensual delight. Or perhaps it was that these objects were seized to liquidate debts. Chickens and communal children squalled among them. The odd beached sailor peered unshaven and dyspeptic out of a window, trying either to remember or forget the night before. On a line strung across the yard hung women's clothes and spattered sheets, reeking of the semen broadsides of a dozen nationalities.

'Payment is a matter of no importance,' said Hauptmann, looking at the guns heaped up in boxes in the centre of the room. 'There will be time for that when you are king, Duke Bosun. In the meanwhile your credit is good.' He had no intention of revealing that he had already been paid for the guns by the French. 'You know that both myself and the French – everyone but the English – are convinced of the legality of your claim. We will support you to enter into what is your right.'

'It be my right,' declared the squat figure emphatically. He stamped his foot and breasts of fat quivered with sympathetic rage.

'Quite so – your right.'

'My father be king. *His* father be slave.'

'So I understand.'

'For why he call himself king?'

'Quite so.'

'His blood no be king's blood.'

'No.'

'His mouth no be king's mouth.'

Hauptmann felt a desperate need to stem this flood of synecdoche. 'There is nothing of the king about him,' he summed up roundly.

'No. His blood be slave blood. His mouth be . . .'

'Concerning the timing of this operation . . . It would be best if King Jack were already dead . . .'

Duke Bosun looked blank and impassive. 'Oh, he be dead for sure. He be dead too much. My ju-ju man chop him fine.'

Hauptmann made a pained face. 'Yes, yes, yes,' he said testily. 'Ju-ju is all very well, Duke . . . *King* Bosun, but perhaps something a little more direct . . . One of his wives perhaps . . .' There was a slight scuffling from outside the door. Hauptmann lumbered across the room and tore it open. Nothing stirred. He toiled down the passage and looked round the corner. The girls were sprawled on chairs, swinging their legs to cool their private parts. They looked up at him with their silly moon faces and giggled. A lizard on the wall made copulatory thrusts with its body. Hauptmann glared and returned to the room.

'It is none the less important that we act quickly. The English are installing an explosives plant. I have seen it with my own eyes – on the Consul's boat.'

Bosun looked up, but could see nothing for the light reflected from the thick lenses of his glasses.

'I will not mince words, King Jack.' Truscot tried to summon a sense of outrage, but felt nothing but overwhelming fatigue. 'It is all these killings over saucy nut. It must stop. If you do not desist at once, I fear I must inform the Consul.'

'But, Reverend . . .'

'No, no. I sabby what you're going to say. It be Akwa fashion, therefore unchangeable. You are an old tree and cannot bend like a young one. But you yourself were the first to change the old, bad way where household slaves went in fear of their lives at the death of a powerful man. The path to improvement is always a rocky one that leads uphill. You reaped the reward of the previous reform. You must not be faint-hearted now.'

'But, Reverend . . .'

'Nor may you argue, as do the old nobility, that you will knock off such old customs when your mother and father are dead, that they were born in one faith and must be allowed to die in it. Owing to your . . . particular circumstances . . . you have no family of birth. There is thus no impediment that might prevent your making a change for the better.'

'But, Reverend . . .'

'Nor is it sufficient to say that you are king here and not I. I am fully aware of your position and my own. But I cannot forbear to tell you the truth and explain God's Law, for you and your people are at risk of eternal damnation, you for whom Our Saviour gave his life gladly.'

King Jack looked suddenly interested. 'For what he die for me? I not know him. When he die? How he sabby I go live bad life?'

Truscot stopped, an old war-horse pulled up short in mid-charge by a command called by the enemy. Surely he had explained this before? Weariness swept over him. He took a deep breath and began the long haul up to enlightenment. 'He died that we might be saved. He died so we could go to Heaven – God's castle.' It was suddenly very hot in here.

'If when you die you go for God's castle and that be damn fine place, why you not kill yourself right now?'

Truscot reeled but plodded wearily on. 'When you send traders out with goods, why don't they hurry home early before your business is done? You would not be pleased. So it is with God. He sends us to this place for his business. He it is who calls us back when the task is done.' He was mumbling now, half visualizing himself still staggering through the forest, ricocheting from one phantom tree to the next.

King Jack clapped and giggled. 'Fine! Damn fine! But you should sabby, Reverend, I no be damn fool you think me be. I no like to kill folks but they must fear me, otherwise they all try to kill me with freemason. So I use saucy nut. My son, John Bull, he make big palaver for market. "How much saucy nut? You sure he kill? You show me with chicken." That way, they all frightened. Not many be killed here. But they fear too much. Fear a friend for me.'

'But this is terrible. You play with fear of death. You are deceived by Lucifer, the Prince of Darkness (*something wrong with the etymology there; never mind, press on*). Think of the innocents slain.'

King Jack flashed an angry look and rattled his trust bracelets as if to recall proofs of probity.

'They no be innocent! Saucy nut only kill those be guilty.'

Prince John Bull intervened. 'You do not understand, Reverend. If they are innocent, they do not die. They vomit up the poison. That is the beauty of it.'

'But that cannot be. It cannot work.'

'It be black man fashion. White man no sabby any thing about it.'

'Forgive me, Reverend. How do you know it does not work? Have you tried it?'

'No, of course not.'

'You are perhaps confused because people sometimes cheat. If you boil the nut, the poison is killed and the guilty go free. If you put ordinary poison in the water, innocent people die and are held to be guilty. This why my father does no trust the ju-ju men.'

'You see ju-ju man here?' demanded King Jack. 'Tell him, John Bull, about ju-ju man.'

John Bull giggled. 'My father played a trick on the ju-ju man. He always distrusts them, having seen whole villages laid waste by their work. He hid a necklace and told everyone it had been stolen. Oh! how he shouted and roared. The women were shaking. The slaves rolling their eyes. Then he sent for the ju-ju man and told him to find out who stole it. King ju-ju ran around staring in bowls of water and chickens' entrails, holding his head and muttering over leg-bones. Then he said he had found the thief and named my father's best slave. He wanted to put him to the poison test and mixed saucy water but my father made him drink it himself.' King Jack guffawed and slapped his leg at the recollection of it.

'What happened?'

They stared at him, a slow pupil. 'But he died, of course. That is the point.'

It is the task of a king to sum up after a discussion and express the feeling of all. King Jack did so now. 'That be proper Akwa fashion. When one man hurt tother, tother must hurt him back worse; and if a third man put in his mouth, shoot him.' He paused, hoping for some acknowledgement of his philosophy but heard none. 'There be different, other palaver, for which *you* must answer to *me*. It my daughter, Adu.'

'Adu? Is she well? But I saw her only the other day, dancing for Mammy Wata. That is another matter on which we must talk, King – her marriage. It is not right that she should be married off to an old man. It no be fit. He has many wives already. God ordained us to take one wife only.'

'Akwa man need many wife. Need many children. He be potentate.'

'*Im*potentate, more like,' thought Truscot, then said, 'But most of his wives – I hazard to say those that are faithful – are without issue.' A sudden image of poor, barren Mary flashed into his mind. 'If children be your purpose, then you should give young women to vigorous young men that your marriages may be fruitful.'

'This no be to this palaver. You teach Adu to read and write. I tell you no. You tell me no be fit she fool woman. Now she in plenty trouble. All your fault.'

'But why? Please tell me what has happened.'

'Now she sabby write, she change book for trade, change all numbers in my store. No one sabby any more how much small men owe me. Book all in her finger. All your fault.'

'But King Jack . . .'

'You no worry, Reverend. I know you friend for Akwa man. I give her good cow-hiding. I say, "Don't you ever do that thing again for ever or I throw you out. You end up in Dufief's house." How your garden?'

Truscot was momentarily nonplussed by this sudden squirish turn of the conversation. 'Alas. Everything we plant comes to nought.'

King Jack looked significantly at John Bull. 'Try again, Reverend. To begin new field be hard. I know for sure, this time your garden will grow.'

I do not hold my trip to the plantations to have been wasted. I have learnt much both concerning the country and the native mind. Also I feel I have a closer understanding with King Jack. He told me at the last that we were to be friends.

Silent Will has also opened his heart to me and declares with great feeling his wish to learn God's book. I have seen his assiduity and resistance to the avocations of sin daily demonstrated in my class. I have discussed it with Mary and we are to send him to the Bible school in Calabar, where he will receive training as a catechist. King Jack does not object, terming him a 'rubbish boy'. I mean to show otherwise.

On the way back to town, coming to the crossing of two paths, I happened across an Ekpo runner, clothed entirely in a raffia costume from head to toe and with his face hidden. He rang his bell at me and raised the whip of green leaves with which they are wont to strike slaves and non-members who do not flee before them. Then, strangely, he touched his head as if in salute and went peacefully on his way.

Hard by the town I encountered Crosby, looking as seedy and unwashed as ever. Having read Dr Skae on the subject, I noted his sallow skin, the dark rings under his eyes and the tremor of his hand – the classic symptoms of an inveterate and unrepentant masturbator. I fear he was in drink, but one cannot encounter sin without encountering sinners, so I greeted him as civilly as I might. Given the association made between drunkenness and godliness in the native mind, he doubtless passes here for a near saint. 'You,' he said, 'will want to see this, a slave market.' I accompanied him, for it is surely wise that in future times, when the lambs have been led to God, they should know 'this is the rock from which we were hewn, the pit from which we were digged.'

I cannot speak of the shamefulness of those poor people and the way they were handled and displayed naked as meat at a country fair, of the rending asunder of families, the cleaving of the bonds of tender feeling. A small boy was sold for fifteen bracelets of copper. I had nearly bought him myself as the only way in which he might be enlarged unto liberty, but I realize that one man cannot set himself alone against this evil. It is too large, its roots go too deep. The way to act is to win men's minds against it.

Such horror was as nothing, however, to that in my heart when I saw him being paid for with the saints' likenesses bestowed upon favoured pupils at my school. To see the pictures of holy intent so perverted to wickedness wrung my spirit and was a timely admonishment against the Popish sin of idolatry into which I had fallen. Yet I will have it stopped! Crosby, of course, rejoiced at my discomfiture, which I found impossible to hide from him.

The 'smokes' have begun. A hot dry wind from the north brings red dust swirling down – some say from the Sahara desert, though certain spores detected by scientific examination suggest it originates much further distant in South America. For weeks on end dust hangs heavy in the still air and simulates the mist of the rainy season. It penetrates everywhere, powdering our clothes and furniture. It is to be tasted in every mouthful of food. It saddens me to see poor Mary, her face swollen, her eyes red as though with grieving, unable to breathe, in wretched misery.

Mary sat on her bed in the daytime night attire of the invalid. Her nose was huge and red, swollen clownishly. It intruded into her vision and made her clumsy, as if all her limbs were sympathetically swollen. It enraged her to be so weak and useless, to be relegated to her room like a broken piece of equipment. Cloths were stuffed into the cracks around the window to exclude the dust, which lay there thick and soft like some crimson form of snow. The heat and stillness of the air suffocated her and made her want to tear open the door and rush outside. She knew that would bring on another seizure. She had to stay here and wait for clearer weather.

Truscot entered and embraced her with mellow affection, dust swirling in after him. 'Mary, how are you? Is there any improvement?'

She smiled weakly. 'It will be better when the dust eases, Mannie. How was the school today?'

He led her to the couch and pressed her to sit. The furnishings had all been shipped from their house in England. It was strange to see them transposed here in this alien setting. As she sat, another puff of dust arose and she began to cough.

'The school is better, much better. Though their opinions remain a little unorthodox. One asked whether, as soon as Akwa people could read and write, God would send them a set of new written commandments for their own so they would not have to use those written for other people.'

Mary felt the urge to laugh but knew she must not. For Mannie this was not a joking matter. She stifled her humour in a cough.

'I am sorry to look so awful, Mannie. It must be terrible to look at my horrid face all swollen like this.'

'Nonsense, my dear.' He smiled and looked at her kindly. 'It makes no difference. It is just as well I did not marry a pretty wife.'

There are some moments that cast a shadow over a whole lifetime. She would never forget this casual remark, intended to be comforting, that so frankly expressed what he really thought of her. She knew it was the truth and that made it unbearable. He might have said that she was still beautiful *to him*. He might have said that he still loved her for all this temporary disfigurement. But now it seemed that she might as well sprout a hump and warts, run with sores, catch leprosy. He would care not a whit the less for her because he gave her the same love as he gave all the world. She began to cry.

'Mary.' He looked at her perplexed. 'What *is* the matter? Sometimes, I fear, I do not understand you at all.'

*

Hauptmann was at that moment many miles beyond the town, ample buttocks constrained in the narrow prow of a native canoe. Behind him was stacked a teetering pile of bottles of squareface gin. Duty in the Lagos colony was higher than in Akwa, so that a regular part of petty trading activity involved the smuggling of gin from one to the other. Most white traders held such enterprise to be beneath them, preferring to abandon it to local men. For Hauptmann, it was a political act of subversion, a guerrilla raid by an irregular. The danger was not acute. There were many hundreds of small channels leading through the swamps and attempting to police them was an act of supreme optimism, the equivalent of firing blindly into the air in the hope of bringing down a bird. Yet it was sufficient to add spice to a trading life. For Hauptmann, it was especially good to win a gamble when the odds were in your favour.

The canoe was drawn up alongside the bank of a minor muddy channel, though the current here flowed steadily, the water the colour of strong tea. Hauptmann drew on a cigarette and leant back on the gin, cursing, as ever, the heat that swamped his chest with dank sweat. The pulla-boys had gone off to a nearby village to buy food before making camp for the night. He would sleep in the boat. Safer from the crawling, slithering things of the night. Earlier, too, they had seen elephants and hippos that came down to wallow. The mosquitoes had begun to whine and the frogs to cark and ping. Where were they? Surely, it was hours since they had left? He hoped there had been no trouble. Come to think of it, it was strange that the whole crew had been neither Krooboys nor Akwans, but Muslims from the north. Krooboys would have tied fishing lines to their toes and caught enough for supper without halting the canoe. Good for the cargo though, for it meant their addiction was to sugar, not alcohol. Still, there could easily have been some bad blood between them and the locals. As he looked at his pocket watch, a mosquito settled and raised its proboscis. His hand descended before the insect could lunge. Damn this heat. A branch snapped and rustled away to the left. They were back, coming through the gloom. There would be a fire. Whatever the heat, they always insisted on lighting a fire. Then there would be singing half the night. The boat bucked, then steadied as the leader stepped on to it. 'You took your time,' Hauptmann growled.

'Sorry, Massa. There were other Akwa men in the village.'

'What?' He turned, surprised by the standard English. 'Who are you? You're not . . . ?' His hand moved slowly towards the Martini-Henry repeater down by the gunwales.

'I think you know me,' said John Bull. A machete gleamed dull metal in the twilight. The blade was imported from Liverpool, but the handle was elegantly carved from local ivory. A steely coolness seemed to pass over the whole river. 'I represent the warriors' society,' he grinned, deliberately imitating a travelling salesman. 'And we wondered whether you would like a demonstration.' The blade swished in the still air. There was a splash and then nothing. Something large and amphibious swished wetly into the river just downstream, greedy to feed. Then there was silence. The boat rocked once more and began to drift back towards Akwa.

Two more twins arrived last night, to the deep joy of Ali, a boy and a girl. We call them Abraham and Sara – to Ali, Ibrahim and Sahara. I remarked to one of the traders how good-natured and happy were the children of Akwa. I never yet heard one cry without good cause. 'It is,' says he, 'the proof that the native's slothful content and mindless indolence is born in him.' I left without another word.

One of the small boys of the school, called Yellow and notable for his mischief more than his diligence, brought me a fish in a large calabash vessel. It seemed rather after the fashion of our native catfish with long whiskers. I thanked him for the kindness and hoped to study it. I should have suspected some impishness from the close attention paid by my class. And, indeed, as soon as touched, it delivered a powerful electric charge fit to take my arm off, so that I was knocked from my chair. Of course, all the pupils found this the funniest thing ever they saw and screamed with laughter in that curious Akwa way. I feel I laughed last, however, for it provided an excellent supper. The people tell me that any number of such fish may live together in a single vessel without mutual harm.

Suddenly, our field produces some green shoots. We should not, of course, yet begin to reckon the size of our harvest, but I do hold this in some sense a good omen. We have ploughed and laboured in the mission field but brought forth no crop. Now, at last, we see the young shoots that may grow up to firm-rooted faith.

Truscot's writing of his journal was disturbed by a peremptory rapping at the door. Rising from his desk, he crossed the room and looked out, for the door was left permanently open, a mark of his availability to the world. It was Nash. Was this peace or war? Truscot offered his hand. Nash ignored it, lumbered past him into the room and sat down. War then. Or perhaps he was just excessively encumbered, with a suitcase under one arm and hat fanning away in the other.

'Pray be seated, Mr Nash.' An opening salvo. 'Is this a social visit or do you seek me out in my pastoral capacity?' Direct hit. Nash smelled slightly of gin. Doubtless it constituted part of his breakfast.

Nash looked briefly bewildered, then, like an old, barnacle-encrusted man-of-war, he slowly brought his guns round to bear. 'It is a trade matter. That is the point. It is not a missionary matter at all, but a trade matter.' He looked for a weakness to assault. 'Do I smell wine, Reverend?'

Truscot blushed. 'A morning dose of quinine wine. That is

all. If you feel the lack of something strengthening, perhaps I might offer you a glass.' Got him there.

'It is not for wine that I am here, Reverend. It is to discuss a financial deception and shameless fraud.' He dumped the suitcase on the floor and flipped open the lid, delving inside to hold up a handful of saintly images, which he shook accusingly. 'I understand that the gullible have been tricked into accepting these as legal tender. I further understand that these were issued by yourself.'

'They were indeed issued by myself, but only for use within the mission. I deplore their use outside the confines of this compound.' There seemed to be an awful lot of them. Surely he had never issued all those?

'But do you realize the consequences? Their effect on prices?'

Truscot lent forward and examined the pictures. Here was a picture of Abraham guarding his sheep. He had never issued Abrahams – or Ibrahims, as Ali would have it. Here was the Virgin Mary, face blank and terribly pale as if after fever. He would certainly never have issued these instruments of Popery.

'Wait! I never gave out these. They are forgeries. Well, perhaps not forgeries, but they have no connection with me or the coupons issued within the mission.'

'Come, come, Reverend. Where else *could* they have come from?'

'I do not know. Someone has deliberately imported them to cause trouble. Who could have done such a thing? Only a trader would have the opportunity. How did you come by these?'

'But you started this, Reverend. I look to you to redeem these notes.' He pushed the case across the floor towards Truscot with his foot. Truscot resisted, so that a sort of urchins' football ensued, both men seemingly tackling each other for possession of the suitcase, like waifs brawling among the debris of a city slum.

'You know I cannot. It would bankrupt the mission. Grunt!'

'If you do not, it will bankrupt trade. Puff' The suitcase under their combined efforts revolved harmlessly, a weather-vane of the winds of war.

'You are deliberately conspiring to undermine the mission.'

'Your sole purpose seems to be to destroy trade and I shall complain to the Consul.'

'I shall write to your owners; you will be dismissed.'

'I shall write to your mission headquarters; you will be recalled.'

They paused, two men of beyond a certain age, red, perspiring, glaring eye to eye, fighting over a suitcase like two railway porters. So, then, war!

'War!' said Duke Bosun angrily. 'They done chop Hauptmann! This be war!' The boat had been found drifting and blood-stained. No trace of the crew remained. They had melted away into the swamps. The gin had been filched by fishermen. (Waste not whatnot, as Prince John Bull would have said.) No body would ever be yielded up by the many mouths and teeth of the river.

Duke Bosun's minions eyed him without enthusiasm. They knew that war in these parts was seldom a glorious head-on confrontation of good and evil, with dashing sallies and heroic feats. It was a matter of skulking raids, catching people unawares and unarmed, killing women and children in preference to men who could fight back. Death came for most not in the heat of battle, but at night when sleeping, or in the chill of dawn while fetching water alone. Still, for some there would be the opportunity of taking cherished warriors' titles. For others, the chance of booty.

'I go catch Jack. I go chain him,' declared Duke Bosun. 'He go crawl at my feet.'

He knew that strategy and planning were all-important. First of all, he would need the proper clothes. He was thinking in terms of a naval campaign. Being upstream, he could embargo Jack's trade and cut him off from markets. Jack would not dare interfere with white men who wanted to trade with him. First things first. He would clearly need an admiral's uniform with gold braid, a plumed hat and a brass telescope 'for fancy' – also guns and powder. It would be best to get a message to the French. A canoe was dispatched by a circuitous route.

The first result of the 'war' was a spectaculr rise in the price of chickens on account of the vast number consigned to perdition to adorn the shrines of interested deities or to meet the needs of diviners. A hundred gods and spirits were consulted and advised. In the settlements of the bloodmen iguanas became an endangered species.

White traders began to dismantle the tenuous causeways that linked their hulks with the mainland, shifting the contents of their sheds aboard, congratulating themselves on not having created an immobile establishment like that foolhardy missionary. On the whole, they had no quarrel with King Jack. He was a sound ruler, who assigned, like them, the highest priority to regular trade. It was unlikely that Bosun would offer more advantageous rates and, since his meeting with the French, he was tarred with the smear of Gallophilia. Their policy was, then, to support Jack without becoming involved themselves, but in return for promised concessions. Their one fear was that trade would be closed. Endless meetings stoked up their fears and coined rumours in the guise of privileged information. The whites were to be massacred. The government planned to declare a British colony. The Consul was on his way with a force of blue-jackets. The Consul could not be found at all. His ship was lost. A French force had been sighted heading down from Marseilles.

Armed guards appeared at the sheds. Traders always had a weapon within reach, a machete under the pillow, a repeater leaning against the veranda rail. War canoes began to manoeuvre on the river, enormous dug-outs some forty feet long with raised gunwales. In the midst of the hulks lurked King Jack's great canoe with two decks, a little castellation being added on top, like some frivolous Thames pleasure boat. The whole was painted in bright colours, yellow and red, with fluttering ensigns and bunting. Lacy fretwork trimmed the roof, shaking beneath the twin impact of two powerful men beating large slit gongs to communicate with smaller vessels operating up to three miles away over the water. At the prow sat King Jack beneath his enormous umbrella, as on Truscot's first day, his silver snuff-box bearer behind him. Strapped to the bows was a large cannon, specially shipped from Birmingham with lesser arms mounted on swivels at the sides. They put on a great display with their thirty paddlers and the massed sharpshooters at the centre. Over all fluttered a huge Union Jack, at once a challenge and a response to Bosun's tricolour.

Wherever it appeared, the vessel was accompanied by gunfire, roars and vigorous drumming from the men and ululations from the women. Even Truscot found it hard to suppress a proud swelling of the breast when he saw it cruising the water, a great curl of white foam at the prow, the paddlers pulling away in time.

Reports circulated of a few ragged skirmishes up in the north. Traders returning from the inland markets had been fired on. Some of King Jack's men had been made prisoner. Duke Bosun was said to have withdrawn to Alligator Island, further up-river and a strategic point from which to enforce a blockade.

And then, quite suddenly one day, the entire fleet had disappeared. The river was bare. The town lay deserted apart from women, children and white men. Chickens wandered unheeded. Shed doors banged in the wind. Women ruled the town. They made hay with the possessions of their menfolk. Whereas normally virtually incarcerated in their compounds, they now roamed the streets in giggling inebriated bands. They took to wearing men's clothes and parading under arms in the street. The few local men fled their sarcastic tongues and licentious ways. Some were flogged by the women with high good humour. The Lady of Misrule was Crashy Jane, formidable in her new power. Until the fleet returned and with it the King, there was no law in Akwa but hers.

A dreadful hush hangs over Akwa town like a denser form of the 'smokes'. I yet pray that the Consul will arrive in time to prevent killing, though I realize this is to live in hope of vigorous action from 'good King Log'. I have offered myself as intermediary, but the only point on which the two parties are unanimous is in their refusal of my services. The weight of fearful anticipation weighs heaviest on poor Mary, who has abandoned herself to a form of nervous prostration. It is only the presence of the twins and Ali – constantly solicitous – that keeps her spirits up at all. I busy myself with the garden – which now flourishes, especially the beans. How unpredictable yet certain at the end is the benison of nature's foison!

Occasionally bands of women come by, both deft girls and the weightier great ladies. They gather and perform charming, lively songs before me, but always with the greatest good humour and the most lively gestures. I never fail to offer them refreshment, of which they are most appreciative. Ali is in terror of them and will not venture out of the yard. Yet Jane and her girls have always been most forthcoming towards me. Moreover, they are greatly in awe of the twins and will not enter the mission. I commended their martial spirit in assuming the burden of the defence of the town but urged restraint upon them, for male and female are as the right and left hands upon the body. What needs a body of two right hands?

At last, news! Prince John Bull has just passed by, tired but content. His greatest concern was not to appear in town in anything less than his usual immaculate condition. The war may be over. It is to be summed up in the words *veni, vidi, fugi*, 'I came, I saw, I fled', for thus did Duke Bosun's troops conduct themselves. It seems they were ambushed by the King, who, cutting across Alligator Island, took them from the rear with total surprise. Scarce had the first volley been fired when Duke Bosun straightaway fled in his canoe, which took the fighting spirit out of his men and opened the way to a parley. Since the King's canoes were at the other side of the island, he was in no position to pursue Duke Bosun, who is now said to be leading a miserable existence in the swamps. It is believed he will have to 'sweet mouth' the King and sue for peace. John Bull was evasive when I asked how many poor souls had lost their lives in this foolish enterprise. 'Small people only,' he declared, 'no men of rank.'

He requested that he might await the arrival of his father at the mission, being still in awe of Crashy Jane and her Amazons, to which I readily consented. He is still little more than a boy and the delicate flower of his innocence must be protected.

The Consul arrived in good time not to have to do anything but a certain amount of posturing. His vessel dropped anchor two days after Duke Bosun's ignominious defeat and he himself was in so complete a state of ignorance concerning developments on the Coast that he was perplexed at the turmoil caused by his firing off a salvo of cannon to announce his coming. The brief and inglorious civil war of Akwa would go unreported in official dispatches. 'War?' he asked. 'What war? Who with? I expect you'll find it was all just a silly rumour. Seen it happen loads of times. Best to say nothing. Only cause a to-do in London, questions, paperwork. Let's have all the chiefs together and have a good jaw. Sort it all out.'

Alas, Scuttlebutt had not made due allowance for the temperament of those involved. He blandly assumed that Duke Bosun, having made a bit of a mess of things, would now creep back to make amends, lose a couple of house-points, take his punishment and carry on as before. Duke Bosun, however, was the scion of noble root-stock. To be sure, it pained him to sit in the mangrove swamps with his downcast supporters. Worst of all was that his entire wardrobe had been lost in the débâcle and the soggy but ornate admiral's uniform in which he now found himself mocked both his past pretension and his present discomfort.

In the forests behind Duketown he had established an arsenal, where were laid down copious supplies of powder and provisions. He avoided passing the main settlement. He knew that the first thought of his rival would be to despoil it and he did not wish to see it reduced to ashes and ruin or encounter the swaggering stragglers of King Jack or the wretched survivors of his own household. Quietly, like a forest creature, he installed himself in his fastness, cursing the French for perfidy, his troops for cowardice – everyone, indeed, but himself. In the arboreal gloom he fell prey to deep depression. It seemed that the only one who remained faithful to him was the guinea-worm that dwelt in his leg.

The King returned to Akwa this morning with drums and trumpets, masqueraders dancing on his great canoe. His vessel entered the harbour with great style, the paddlers bending to their labour and at the last moment executing a great, smooth curve to avoid a collision with the consular vessel. I accompanied John Bull to greet his father, but as our canoe drew near I was appalled to see the cluster of human heads affixed to the prow of the vessel, like bumpers to ward off collision. While congratulating him on his safe return, I felt obliged to voice my displeasure at this gory spectacle. I remarked that the human anatomy was not designed by God to provide baubles for his boat. For some reason he took this as very funny. Crosby, in his godlessness, made some remark about my perhaps preferring foreskins after the Old Testament fashion – whereby he showed his ignorance, since all Akwa men are circumcised.

Big palaver aboard the Consul's ship. Scuttlebutt, I suspect at the beck of the traders, sought to punish King Jack for interrupting trade and so violating his treaty. He wished to reduce 'comey', the impost payable to the King for the right to open trade, in return for their 'loyalty'. I spoke in defence of King Jack and cited the mischief of the French and the injudicious trade in arms as lying at the root of present troubles. The traders muttered among themselves but could not contradict me. If the wolf would eat the sheep, he must first destroy the watch-dog.

King Jack wished the Consul to execute Duke Bosun or, at the least, exile him to Fernando Poo in perpetuity, being unwilling or unable to terminate the war until he might be yielded up to justice. As I feared, Duketown has been laid waste and many of the roofs of Akwa will be refurbished with metal sheeting from Bosun's palace. Yet to spoil an African town is a small matter. It may be re-erected again in less time than it takes to knock it down. I stressed the need to stop the killing, yet I feel that if the execution of Bosun is the only way, then that route should be followed with purpose.

At this point a messenger came to say that Bosun has fallen prey to melancholy, has betaken himself to his arsenal, knocked out the heads of half a dozen kegs of powder and sits upon them, a box of matches in his hand, threatening to blow himself and all about him to Kingdom Come.

Such is apparently often the case with the mighty of Akwa and persons cited to me other similar events that have occurred in the past. There is clearly a melodramatic streak in the character of the race. The first wife of a previous monarch, having established the transfer of her husband's affections, did likewise and thus destroyed half the town, most effectively clearing the site whereon the present King's house was subsequently erected. We must be grateful that

Bosun sits in the forest and can only make hay with the trees and monkeys.

Scuttlebutt, doubtless fearing that such a detonation would involve at least reports in London, ordered Bosun summoned, but it is clear he will not come and deliver himself into their hands without further parleys. At the end it was decided to fine Duke Bosun a large quantity of palm-oil, but it seems far from clear how he may hope to pay such a sum given his present circumstances.

Nash, peevish and upsettish as ever, produced his tired old suitcase of holy images like a huckster at a fair and sought to embroil the Consul in the business. Having argued it back and forth, I found myself amazed to hear Scuttlebutt make a Solomon-like pronouncement – but such indeed was the case.

'I really see no need to concern ourselves with the redemption of these pictures against copper manillas – on the highest possible authority. England is the only modern nation with convertible paper money to adhere to the gold standard. I read in *The Times* that even here there is dispute with the Governor of the Bank supporting a non-convertible paper. If the Bank of England is no longer to pay a bearer of its banknotes in gold, why should the Reverend do so in manillas?' Palaver set.

'More food, John Bull? In the ships you cannot have eaten well.' Ali spooned more mutton *rendang*, aromatic with musky spice, on to the plate and pushed it back to John Bull.

'Thank you. In the boats there was no good food. Even the warriors' feast after the battle was not good. The flesh of children and young people is too sweet.' He studied Ali's face, looking him in the eyes, then guffawed. 'No, brother Ali. I am joking. Akwa men cannot eat each other. That is only for foreign enemies. It would be like sleeping with our own sisters.' The marinaded mutton fell apart to the touch of his finger. He formed it into a neat bolus and popped it into the O of his smiling mouth. 'Does Reverend Truscot eat this food?'

Ali shook his head. 'No. Like all white men, he and *ibu* eat from tins. Real food is too strong for them. Only on Sundays do I make him proper food like this. Eaten every day this food would make him too hot and passionate. He could not continue as a God-man.' He swelled his chest and stuck out his jaw aggressively. They giggled like schoolboys at the thought of Reverend Truscot engaged in a passionate act, hugging each other in laughter that grew the stronger for being stifled.

'The only problem,' gasped Ali at length, 'is that all the labels come off the tins because of the damp.' He indicated a row of blank, gleaming cans on a shelf above them. 'We never quite know what it is we are opening, though the Reverend has become expert in distinguishing different kinds of foods by the noise they make when you shake the tin.' This sent them off into further paroxysms of giggles, John Bull miming a man shaking and listening with mouth agape. Finally, weak from laughter, Ali wiped his eyes on the hem of his sarong and tried to turn to more serious matters while he could yet breathe.

'What will happen to Duke Bosun now?'

'He will crawl back into Duketown and try to build it up again. He will start to buy slaves to enlarge his house and replace the men he lost. We will sell him some of ours – not the best – but it would be wise to have our eyes and ears in that house. You understand, we have too many enemies to the north who would like to chop us to allow Bosun house to disappear. We must keep Akwa strong. He will bide his time. One day he will try to avenge his house.' He shrugged. 'It is the Akwa way.'

He chewed in relative silence for a while, the regular churn of his jaws becoming just another sound of nature, like the waves on a beach or the wind in the trees.

'Most of my men were Muslims from the north,' he said reflectively. 'The Consul's soldiers come from there too. It seemed to me they were braver than Akwa men. They did not run away as soon as there was shooting. They did as they were ordered. They were not afraid to die. Tell me something of your God, brother Ali. Perhaps it is something I should know.'

While John Bull received instruction in the Muslim faith in his kitchen, Reverend Truscot sat on the veranda, greeting passers-by in the easy, friendly way that marks a man as a neighbour. At his feet crouched James and John, not the sons of Zebedee, intent upon the pursuits of the young. James was examining a fly with deep wonder. John clutched a handful of grass and experimented in throwing it away, always forgetting to open his clenched fingers at the essential moment and sitting down heavily. Truscot sipped a glass of quinine wine and read again the letter open on his lap. It was from Silent Will.

Dear Reverend and Mother Truscot,
Too long I live here and no write. But my heart so full of sadness when I think of you, I cannot send letter which I now do. A brother from Akwa will bring you this letter since he must return to look for his people and oil lamps after the war palaver. Life here is very hard, all our seed being spilled upon the stony ground. You tell me the Lord is my dwelling-place and indeed I have no other. Another Akwa brother has taken me in for that the missionaries vex with me and throw me from their house. Do not believe the lies spread by malicious mongers of rumours. The truth is simple. I was entertaining a sister in my room for prayer meeting and Bible discussion. It is so hard to know the way of the Lord. Since I have been here I have learnt many new sins that I thought before to be all right. I am telling her of all these sins and urging her steps to the right when others are telling lies to the missionaries about me. Also they say I drink which never was true.

Now the woman with child and say I am the father, which cannot be true because I never lied with her and anyway I am not the only one. All the boys here lie with her – even those from her own house which no be right as it say in the Bible. So how she know I be the father? So I get angry and go to her house and break her mirror and now she make big palaver about the mirror and say I must pay for it and her brother make much trouble for me and he hit me till all my body hurt. All the time I am looking to the Bible for guidance, like you tell me, and weeping and sighing and repenting.

So I hope you will please send me money, also new shoes – the kind with elastic sides – since those I had are now wore out, also a watch and a new hat so I can go to Church and not feel shame. For it is you who send me to the wilderness. I hope you are very well and Mother Truscot too and maybe she is with child, I hope so and that only the servants of the Devil that you don't like die from the war and that in very great pain and suffering. Also send walking cane, the one with glass top.

Your brother on the Cross,

Silent Will

Truscot sighed. The twins, sated on the milk of the Sierra Leone woman, belched. Silent Will seemed indeed to have found a voice, but not his own. His enormous progress in orthography had been matched by a decline in moral vigour and the acquisition of a slothful materialism that seemed endemic at points of European influence. It was a sickness as pernicious and debilitating as any purveyed by Monsieur Dufief's establishment. Before European contact the Akwans must surely have possessed almost all known vices. To this, Westerners had added the fatal ingredient of hypocrisy. It was the mistake of following on the heels of traders instead of moving in ahead of them to prepare the people for their deadly impact. He was like a physician who had come too late to engage in proleptic vaccination. The patient was already mortally infected.

A woman passed by, suckling a child as she walked, the breast jouncing and bouncing about the child's mouth. It was a large child and regarded the twins with cow-like, incurious eyes. The woman, however, looked at them with dread, thanking whatever deity she favoured for having delivered *her* from such a fate. Out here, children continued to nurse at the breast until four or five years old, a natural form of limiting the fertility of the people. A wave of musky odour swept after her, rank but somehow not disagreeable, the smell of humanity on the Coast. It had nothing to do with cleanliness or race. After a few weeks in this climate it descended upon all like a universal benefaction. Truscot had become aware of it lurking with guilt-inspiring tenacity in his own armpits. No amount of washing could remove it. The traders' habit of dousing themselves with cologne only made it worse. He knew that, like fever and tropical pallor, it would disappear only once one was on the blue water.

Truscot's garden stretched, verdant, the other side of the path, an advertisement for European notions of order. In the plantations the Akwa sowed yams in tidy mounds, but over time these gave way to rank growth and more delinquent arrangements. Truscot's garden was neatly raked and well-watered, the beans twining dexterously up tripods of firm canes. A trim fence some five feet in height deterred goats and iguanas, though since the war the latter had been blessedly reduced in number. It pleased him to have done most of the work himself, though neighbours had assisted with the clearing and he was sure he had seen shy old ladies helpfully watering his crops at night. It was this community of endeavour, surely, that had contributed to the eventual success of the garden.

It was the part of the day most conducive to content. The sun behind its shield of dust produced brilliant smears of red and gold that were picked up and reflected back by the sea. The diminishing light lent enchantment to the raw scars inflicted by human hand and made poverty picturesque. Beauty in Africa, thought Truscot, was always from nature, never from Man's activity. The twins clutched stickily at Truscot's legs. James (or was it John?) began to eat his grass.

At the edge of the clearing a young man appeared, clad in a check sarong, apparently unhurried, as if returning home from his evening bath. He strolled up to the fence and stopped in a curiously English way, as if for a chat about marrows. He saluted Truscot, 'Welcome.' Then, quite suddenly and looking only slightly surprised, he fell down dead. James, or perhaps John, clapped and laughed at this fine trick. At first Truscot thought the man had been shot and waited for the bang as one does when seeing the puff of smoke from a discharged weapon at a distance, knowing the sound will follow.

He leapt to his feet. 'Ali! Ali!' Ali emerged, circumspect as a householder roused at midnight, John Bull towering over him from behind. Seeing the prostrate form, they ran over. Ali gathered up the children and hurried them away, James doing vigorous imitations of the falling swoon he had just witnessed. 'Careful, Reverend,' cautioned John Bull in a low voice, 'there is yellow fever in town.'

'Yellow fever? How? When?' Shamefully, he heard the fear in his own voice.

'It came on a ship a week ago. No one knew. Now the bodies are too many.'

'Perhaps it is a mistake. It could be malaria. You cannot be sure.'

The Prince shook his head. 'White men to die like this, maybe. But Akwa people, too, are caught. It is a bad sickness and a bad time to come like this during the smokes.' He stirred the dead man with his immaculate shoe. 'We must get rid of this body.'

'But how? Will you assist me?' He stooped to lift the corpse, but John Bull seized his arm. 'Be careful, Reverend! We cannot do it ourselves. It is too dangerous.'

'How then?'

The Prince stared blankly. 'We shall make some slaves do it, of course. Best we don't tell them what he died of. Otherwise we have to whip them to make them do this thing.'

'Prince John Bull, that is immoral!'

'You cannot leave it outside your door. Look!'

Truscot had never wondered before why yellow fever was so called. He had imagined it to be due to jaundice-like symptoms induced by the disease. But the deceased had looked relatively normal. In death, on the other hand, decomposition was almost supernaturally fast, as if offering an accelerated display for the instruction of the curious. Truscot had encountered the dead in many forms in the exercise of his trade, the bloated, featureless horrors fished, eight days old, from the harbour, the desiccated cadavers of the very old, the indecently succulent corpses, full of blood, of mothers dead in labour. Never, however, had he seen one change so rapidly in colour before his eyes. As he watched, the dark flesh tones gave way to bright yellows and oranges that flowed through it as if in emulation of the sunset raging briefly above. The whole cadaver seemed to collapse on itself as though only a shell and exuded a strong smell of old flatulence. This would not do. He must organize.

'Help me wrap the body. We can use the ju-ju curtains.' That, at least, would be one problem solved.

John Bull was scandalized. 'That cloth in the bad bush? It is for the honourable dead alone. No be fit! *That* is immoral.'

Truscot refused further discussion. He called to Ali to fetch an old sheet from the house and he and John Bull rolled the detumescent remains on to it, fastidious as old maids in avoiding contact with bare flesh. Then they shambled, hobbled, limped the half mile down to that end of the copse that was still 'bad bush', barking their shins on the deceased as they went, looking like schoolboys on a jape tossing one of their fellows in a blanket.

'This be far enough. We leave him here.' Without more ado Prince John Bull curtly dropped his end of the burden at the foot of a low bush and began to wipe his hands enthusiastically on the grass. Truscot was left foolishly holding half the body, becalmed like the rear end of a pantomime horse. Every Christian feeling declared this to be an unreasonable way to treat a fellow mortal, but he knew John Bull had metaphorically as well as literally washed his hands of the matter. There was no more to be done.

They walked back towards the mission, the sunset now a thing of horror. 'What precautions have been taken? Have you quarantined the ship?'

'Too late for that now, Reverend. The yellow jack will be on every ship in the harbour by the end of the week, more common than the Union Jack. We must each take our own precautions. If I were you, I close the school for a while. It will be a good time for the ju-ju men.'

Looking back, John Bull saw a small, naked boy rushing triumphantly towards the town bearing a rare treasure in his hand, the old sheet from the mission, plucked from the rotting corpse. John Bull shrugged. It was each man for himself now.

The fever settled most heavily, as is always the case, upon the poorer, more populous sections of the town, fattening itself for an assault against the bastions of the wealthy. It raged among the slave quarters, gathering victims from male and female populace alike. Space in the 'bad bush' was in short supply, most victims not qualifying for proper burial, so that rich and poor jostled each other promiscuously for position, the carrion teeming and gorging about them. While the Reverend Truscot preached of the day when the wolf would lie down with the sheep, here crocodile contested with vulture and crab with wild dog. The devilish cries at night and the stench during the hours of torrid heat made him repent of the site of the mission. Cloths, soaked in disinfectant, were draped around the fence to keep the disease-provoking miasma away.

Mary, however, seemed to gather strength from the crisis and she drew upon her seasoned competence to meet the demands thrust upon her. She had a job to do, something bigger than herself. She put Mannie's wounding words behind her and spurred herself to gratitude for the good things of this life. The plague must be regarded as one of these. For the first time in months she was able to leave the house, accompanied by Ali, ministering unsparingly to the needy – a cache of whom were conveniently to hand on the edge of the 'bad bush'.

Here dwelt a camp of miserable cast-off women and freed slaves in rickety structures of woven mat and sticks. Too old or ugly for employment by Monsieur Dufief, they gleaned a living in fishing and trading or making the flimsy osier frames on which fish were smoked for sale. Having been disowned by Akwa for real or imagined wrongs, they none the less maintained their allegiance to the traditional morality that had condemned them and vigorously disapproved of and distrusted each other. Old ladies were stern in their reproval of the young wives whose only crime was to have left the yard without their husband's permission. Young wives were roused to indignant contempt for old ladies who were accused of witchcraft. Common adversity did not seem to unite them. It spread and ramified along the fissures of their own internal divisions.

The fever reached them early, probably owing to their frequent trips to the market to sell mangrove oysters. The first to succumb was Joan Green, a strong, young woman. Mary found her abandoned to her suffering and with only the strength left to curse her fellow mortals.

The shelter was filthy and verminous. Cockroaches waved tentative feelers at her from the walls. Her flesh crept at their imagined touch. The alternative name for yellow fever is black vomit. According to the state of the floor, it was fully justified. Goose-pimples still trembled all over Mary's flesh, but she knew where her duty lay. Ali shuddered and ducked in after her. He had a certain knowledge that he could not die as long as he wore the amulet containing a scrap of the Koran about his neck. He stroked it as Mary stroked the fevered brow.

'Knock that off! Head fit to burst.'

'I'm sorry,' said Mary. 'Would you like some broth?'

'Only one thing help Joan. It live for squareface bottle.' She could only be about twenty-five years of age but her skin was already coarse and thick, the hair neglected. Neglect of one's hair was the first sign in Akwa of withdrawal from society. If an Akwan, Mary thought, she herself would be sporting a wild and raddled coiffure.

'I am afraid I have no spirits. Try a little of this.' She ladled the broth into a spoon and tipped it with firm insistence into Joan's mouth. She would learn from this. In future the broth would be kept in an old gin-bottle. Christianity had always used the familiar to destroy it from within.

'It be fool fashion. Nothing save Joan.'

'Nonsense, Joan. As long as you can take nourishment and water and are young and strong, you have a very good chance of surviving the fever.'

'I no be sick of fever alone. It be freemason.' Mary had a

sudden image of an illness that afflicted sufferers with beards and the sprouting of aprons. Of course, she meant witchcraft.

'For what I be sick when other women no be sick? All women here live together. We eat one food. We live for one place. Why I get sick and no they? It be freemason for sure.'

It was commonly accepted in Akwa that yellow fever was a 'white man's disease' brought by, and best treated by, white men. However, the randomness of its incidence was an affront to local reason. It did not seem logical that one person in a family should be struck down while others were not. Whereas Europeans shrugged their shoulders at this point and spoke of random 'luck' or 'the will of God', Akwans pursued explanation with sterner logic.

'It be freemason,' declared Joan firmly. 'It be that woman Aro. She use freemason before to spoil my fishing. She jealous of my beauty. One, two, three day I go for swamp. No catch nothin'. Next time, damn alligator try catch me. Then I know be freemason. Last time, she get away free. This time, I make her drink saucy water.' She spoke with the satisfaction of one whose worst fears about the world are confirmed.

'Beauty?' thought Mary. 'What fools we all are. What a stupid woman. Here she lies dying and all she can think of is her supposed beauty and her spite. Surely there are more important things?'

Joan suddenly threw her head to one side and vomited with an active participation in the event that suggested she was enjoying it. The broth had only been inside her a matter of minutes but in that time, observed Mary, it had already turned black.

'Yes,' gasped Joan Green. 'This time I catch her. She chop nut. She die.' A smile of ghastly content set itself upon her caked lips.

*

Henry Scuttlebutt knew that the dignity of his office would not allow him to flee Akwa in its greatest need. Nothing, however, prevented his imposition of a rigid quarantine. All the sailors ashore were ordered to remain there for the foreseeable future and sought out lodging at Monsieur Dufief's, where they delivered themselves over to slower-chewing spirochaetes. All those still aboard were forbidden any contact with the shore. It was vigorously debated among the crew which half were the more, and which the less, fortunate.

The Consul sat in his deck-chair on the forecastle deck reading grimly in his medical book. 'Yellow fever begins with pains in the loins and a torpor of all the faculties, accompanied by white and greenish vomiting, to which complete prostration succeeds. The vomit then becomes blackish. There may be a brief period in which the patient feels recovered but this is a sign of the approach of death. So rapid is the decomposition of the body that it becomes black and yellow.' He had encountered the disease on the Coast before, in his time as a ship's surgeon. Its apocalyptic quality still awed him. Remedy there was none, the disease being generated from the primal miasma of the waters. About 10 per cent of those infected would survive. All the rest would perish. A rating appeared at his elbow and saluted.

'Excuse me, sir, message from Mr Crosby.'

'Message? You didn't let him aboard, surely? I left strict instructions . . .'

'Yes, sir, begging your pardon, sir. One of his boys called from the canoe. Mr Crosby sends his compliments, sir, and regrets to inform you that he is ill, sir. Since there is no ship's surgeon in the port at the moment, he wondered whether you might be able to assist him, sir.' This was not quite the message given either by Crosby to his boy ('Say him he get off big arse and come here one time or I come catch 'im and cowhide 'im.') or by his boy to the rating ('Massa vex with Consul. Sickness live for him. If Consul no come, he go chop me for sure.'). Damn that man! He was a Consul, not a surgeon. Not much he could do anyway. Hard to refuse outright though. He rubbed his chin reflectively.

'Tell him . . . tell him the Consul (*that'll show him – intimidation through the third person*) regrets but he must be seen to be as subject to the quarantine as is anyone else. It is therefore impossible for him to leave the ship in the interests of good naval discipline.'

He scanned the rating's face for signs of contempt and derision but found none. Years of consular service had entirely suppressed the expression of such emotions.

The fever continues to make inroads on us all. Curiously, Duketown is almost entirely spared the plague. I would attribute this to its almost total isolation following the defeat of Duke Bosun's military ambitions. However, Prince John Bull and the others invoke the witchcraft revenge of Bosun as the explanation of the fever and are said to be spending a fortune employing ju-ju men to turn the freemason back on its originator, a complex and specialized task it appears. Yet others would see in this the divine purposes of God, creating equilibrium and balance in all about him. Personally, I feel divine purposes are like to be a little more inscrutable than such simple visions and put them down wherever I encounter them.

Hearing that Crosby was struck down by the plague, I found myself in a moral dilemma. Should I visit him or no? Our past relations would seem to preclude friendly intercourse. To seek him out in adversity savours of pernicious gloating. Yet, the shepherd must deal with the wolf as well as the sheep. The ungodly are sometimes especially close to the Redeemer at the end. Thus, prepared to be rebuffed, but hopeful of a better success, I made my way through the town to his sheds and persuaded his boatman to convey me to his hulk. The suspension of commerce was a pitiful thing to see. Where once laboured hundreds, the quays and sheds now stand empty and bereft of animation. Most people have betaken themselves to their homes and clapped themselves up until the reign of terror is over. Everywhere are chickens suspended alive to the doorways until their suffering shall cease with starvation. The simple people hold these to be a protection against the illness and allow no man to touch them until their corpse drops rotten to the ground. Also distressed to see the number of dogs inclaustrated alive about the settlement in the expectation that they will attract the malady unto themselves. Such is the folly of popular belief that leads the credulous to actions that surely must increase the risk of infection, already high. One curious Akwan belief: John Bull tells me the local people do not hold malaria to be spontaneously generated from the miasma but to involve hostile water spirits that come out at evening in the form of mosquitoes. The credulous hold that they may avoid the illness simply by keeping away from the swamps at dusk or protecting themselves from the insects with smoke!

The disorder of his accommodations showed that Crosby's servants expected no rapid improvement. I could hear him railing against them from the next room. However, they stood by him faithfully enough and I spoke to them encouragingly, commending their extraordinary courage in setting their lives at such terrible risk by their continued fidelity. They seemed moved by my description of the final stages of the disease and my violent injunctions to avoid contact with the body should mortality eventuate.

Crosby bore the marks of the fever that had wracked him. It was as if his face had come to bear the wounds inflicted on his soul by his life of sin. He seemed touched by my solicitude, but churlishly refused to leave his bed and kneel with me in prayer on the grounds of his infirmity. I remarked that if he had strength to curse his servant, then he had strength to praise the Lord. He requested me to take charge of his last will and testament, there being none other that he could trust, and to undertake to dispense small sums to children he may have sired upon ladies of the town. All this I was glad to do, but urged upon him the need to prepare himself for his end and the meeting with his Maker. Here the fever must have touched his mind, for he grew abusive and accused me of seeking to take advantage of his abstraction to seize his soul. Then, of a sudden, he was all weakness and humility, embracing me and asking forgiveness, yet with an expression of such bare malice upon his face that – unworthy thought? – I wondered if he were not seeking proximity in the deliberate hope of communicating his sickness to me. A missionary need not become totally blind in order to lead others towards the light. I urged him to regain a manly fortitude and promised to come again, leaving certain interesting tracts by his bedside.

Curiously, as I left, I perceived all but one of his domestics fleeing with the better part of his wardrobe and china to the shore; however, thought it no part of my errand of mercy to trouble him further with such intelligence.

The epidemic continued into the next month. Still the smokes filled the air with dust and heat and clamped a perspiring hand over Akwa, so that breath itself was an effort. No stir of wind refreshed the flagging spirits of the inhabitants. As many died from saucy water as from the disease, as old grudges found expression in accusations of freemason. Mary's camp of cast-off women was all but obliterated by its own internal hatreds. Crosby recovered from what revealed itself to be a case of mere malaria and wrote to the Consul complaining that Truscot had incited his boys to mutiny, theft and desertion. Since his hulk was technically a vessel, he sought confirmation of his right to invoke nautical law and hang the offender personally. It made no odds. Scuttlebutt had taken to burning all letters from the shore as a health precaution.

Then, quite unexpectedly, an unseasonable rain rushed in piratically from the sea and washed down upon the town. It hammered the metal roofs stripped from Duketown, swirling away red dust. Big, heavy drops, the temperature of blood, glued the soil to the yards and streets. In Truscot's garden the plants were torn from their trellises and crushed into the mud while those that remained erect were stripped of leaves. Incautious spiders that had confidently installed themselves in gutters and drains were tumbled, in their hundreds, like knots of black wool, into the creeks and channels. In King Jack's castle the rosy, iron cheeks of Queen Victoria gasped and gouted a pure and cleansing vomit from every corner of the building. Children rushed out and danced naked in the spume, their faces streaming with pure unalloyed joy. Iguanas licked it gratefully from their snouts. Truscot had an urge, which he did not resist, to go outside and stamp in a puddle for the sheer pleasure of watching the red water splash up his leg. Looking up in shame, he saw Mary standing at the door laughing happily at him and laughed back.

'There is,' he explained, 'something of the child in all of us. Suffer little children ...' It suddenly occurred to him, how attractive she was looking these days. She seemed to spend less time fretting over her appearance but the result was not an increase in her dowdiness. It was as if she had sloughed off the need to concern herself with such things as a butterfly sloughs off the carapace of its caterpillar body. Ali and Mary brought out armfuls of assorted children and pointed out to them the finer points of rainfall, turning their own faces towards the heavens to receive the blessing of the warm moisture.

Prince John Bull stood in his yard looking at the same heavens and let the weather flow over him, indifferent to the ruin of his coiffure.

The sudden downpour washed and purged the town, scoured out the sour recesses in which the disease dwelt and flushed it away into the sea. A curiously unspoken but universal and unquestioned knowledge spread that the epidemic was over.

King Jack watched the water gouting from the gargoyles of his castle with the quiet satisfaction of every householder who finds his roof in good order in a storm. He smiled down from the balcony to see his son strong and healthy after this terrible time. 'John Bull. You come in now before you catch cold. Hot rain be dangerous. I need to talk with you.' He settled in a mouldering plush armchair by the balustrade and looked out on the rain knifing among the barrels ranged along the waterfront. There was a bleating, followed by an agonized cough from the shelter in the yard where the new ju-ju king was turning back the sickness on Duketown.

The Prince appeared in the doorway, soaked and grinning. He crouched respectfully at his father's feet. Trickles of rain began to flow down his skin and drip on to the floor. The King broached a bottle of squareface gin on the table beside him, poured a glassful and carefully sloshed some over the edge on to the boards. Then he drained it, inverted it and handed it to his son.

'News from Duketown,' said the King and watched him.

'Good news?'

'Good news. This ju-ju king be better than ju-ju king before.'

'Duke Bosun be dead?'

The King smiled regretfully. 'No. Duke Bosun no be dead – yet. His sister, Iyalla, she done die.' He eased a buttock off the chair and broke wind with satisfaction.

'Close, then.' John Bull looked out of the window towards the shelter with respect in his gaze.

'This can profit us, boy. This can help us fine.'

Puzzlement showed on the boy's face. 'How, fadder? How it help us?' He wiped the moisture from his brow so that it now began to drip from his fingers.

'I show you. We chase him. We catch him. But I no can do it myself. I no want other war with Bosun. We use English to fight our war for us. We need your friend the missionary.'

*

The school has been reopened and great was our pleasure to hear Akwan voices raised in song once again and we were pleased to see new pupils among the throng. Also I have begun to go about the town and plantations addressing the people, who now know me by sight and need to know me better. It is a time for new beginnings and fresh hope. Having weathered the war and the epidemic, we are come to feel accustomed here for it is suffering in a place that lends force to the feeling of belonging.

Yet the old ways cling on, like ivy to the rock. We have just heard that Duke Bosun's sister, Iyalla, an old lady firm set in her godlessness, has perished of old age. I fear the worst. John Bull tells me that he is sure they will try to kill slaves for her, as if there were not already enough dead people in the town of Akwa this year. If so, then I shall pursue this matter with all possible vigour through the Consul. Such action is against the treaties signed with the British and I agree with John Bull that it must be punished with the full rigour of the law.

King Jack has launched his great canoe for the funeral and will travel to Duketown to fire a salute on the last day of the interment to show that Duke Bosun is regarded as his powerful subject. This recalls all too closely certain incidents in the past war and it is to be hoped it will not lead to trouble. The differences between them are as yet uncompounded and unatoned. No treaty of peace has been signed. Prince John Bull explains that there will be much feasting before the lady is laid to rest under the floor of her sitting room. Curiously, so great is the awe of things English that the big men of Akwa offer bully beef and ship's biscuit, sometimes cake and preserves – the whole washed down with hot, sweet tea – on the shrines of the relevant deities. The lady, it seems, is to be buried in an English gown and bonnet, together with her best china! Correct usage demands that her second-best china be dashed against the wall after the festivities, the part apparently that slaves enjoy best. As I know from recent events, there *is* something of the schoolboy left in all of us.

Preparations for the funeral proceeded calmly, as if one act of collective grief were being made to serve for all the unrecorded dead of the past few months. An irregular stream of yams and goats flowed towards the ruin of Duketown, swelling to a spate of gin and bully beef as the day drew nearer. Duke Bosun began to erect hasty quarters for his people.

Then the trouble began. Rumours began to circulate around the town that slaves had been led off into the swamp and never been seen again. The bloodmen began to meet in the plantations. During his addresses to the people, more and more questions were asked of Truscot concerning the slaying of slaves.

'My attitude is the same as that of your King,' he replied. 'A slave has the right to just and fair treatment, above all not to be killed for no fault.' King Jack heard these words and approved them.

Noting Truscot's consideration for slaves, when in dispute with their masters they began to flee to the mission for sanctuary. King Jack watched with close attention and was delighted that Truscot urged them to return to their masters. If they feared for their lives or claimed to have suffered excessive punishment, he brought them to the King and asked that he should put them under his personal protection. King Jack was content.

Then the killing began in earnest. Duke Bosun's troops made a surprise raid on one of the outlying plantations, scooping up victims to do honour to Iyalla. The first Truscot knew of it was the appearance of an armed band outside his gate. Brushing aside Mary's pleadings to the contrary, he strode out and demanded to know who they were and what business they had outside the mission.

They looked at him with blank, hooded eyes, chewing on sticks to still their hunger.

'We be bloodmen, Reverend. We no look for war. All we ask is big men hold to laws of Akwa. Slave no longer be chop for no thing. We no hurt no man but we no go home before Duke Bosun done punished.'

He approved their proceeding and fed them in his kitchen. The bloodmen were as good as their word and lined the streets, molesting no one, but were sinisterly omnipresent, examining their weapons or picking on their filed teeth with knives. They took over the smithies and could be heard hammering iron and rasping files far into the night with as much dedication as Adu when making her bangles. The warriors' society similarly took the field, drawing up their ranks in King Jack's yard. It was the moment to take time by the forelock and call a palaver with the Consul.

Duke Bosun had been reluctant to come. Akwa was distasteful to him. Greeting King Jack would be a difficult diplomatic moment. They had not met since the war. At the end of that the usurper Jack had sent him a set of chains with the message, 'You say you go chain me. Come!' He had decided to sit tight and ignore the invitation to the Consul's vessel.

The British Consul, however, was no society hostess and was not above putting an invitation with great insistence. By the curious logic that governed relations in the Delta, Bosun's failure to accept immediately was regarded as 'an insult to the British flag' and Scuttlebutt had ordered a cannon to be fired off over Duketown. When that elicited no response, the muzzles of the guns had been levelled at the town itself, causing a pregnant pause to hang over the whole Coast. Duke Bosun had appeared hurrying down to his boat at once, his clothes in disarray, buckling on his sword as he went.

The meeting was to be held on deck, a large canvas awning having been suspended from the rigging to furnish shade. Chairs had been provided for the grandees, benches for their supporters. Anything not screwed to the deck had been judiciously removed. The last meeting with the chiefs on board had led to the disappearance of all the fire buckets.

The demonstration of precedence was a major art form amongst the chiefs of the Coast. The Consul had assured himself of a dais with a portrait of Queen Victoria mounted above it so that her gimlet-eyed gaze bored into the chiefs and unsettled them. Any human image in this region had connotations of witchcraft and dark power. They shifted uneasily in her presence. The Consul, moreover, was the only one to have a table before him, on which were displayed the instruments of literacy and the Consul's plumed topi, together with a little ivory gavel with which he punctuated the decisions of the court. The handle served the less formal function of fitting neatly into the consular ear for cleaning purposes in moments of distraction. By his left hand lay a pure white handkerchief, spotted with oil of lavender against the smell of the Akwan armpit. At either end of the front wall stood an immobile Hausa soldier in the blue uniform and pill-box hat of the coastal constabulary. On their shoulders leaned highly polished rifles, the gleaming stocks the same colour as their faces. Like many small men, the Consul set great store by the trappings of rank.

The King was seated in the front row of the body of the court. He had assumed a formal pose, hands spread nonchalantly on the arms of his chair. He was sulking, as the Consul had ordered his large umbrella removed. At his feet sat Prince John Bull wearing a sailor suit and boater but experiencing problems with his sabre in such a posture.

On the other side of the aisle sat Duke Bosun, slumped under the weight of his Spanish gold epaulettes and stove-pipe hat. He seemed shrunk and wizened, his single eyebrow somehow stronger and more luxuriant than before, as though it was sucking all the life from his body in its own useless growth. His ju-ju man crouched in a pose mirroring that of John Bull. Unlike the Prince, however, he wore in his hair the feather of the vulturine fish eagle, which bobbed and swooped as if still attached to the bird as he fretted with the gris-gris and amulets that were slung around his bare torso.

The second row, in turn, were considerably inconvenienced by the headgear of the first and many squatted rather than sat on the benches provided.

The traders had dissociated themselves from this local hierarchy by forming a little coterie of their own at an angle to the rest of the court and huddled together in damp cotton suits, fanning themselves with hats and surreptitiously circulating hip-flasks.

Reverend Truscot had not known where to sit and had withdrawn at an angle opposed to that of the traders. He was in full evangelical black, a broad hat resting on his knees, a cane grasped in both hands. Ali sat at his feet and exchanged glances with John Bull.

Past experience suggested the prudence of confiscating firearms on entry and they were stacked at the rear together with King Jack's disconsolately collapsed umbrella. Two horny-handed tars supervised them, illogically quite unarmed.

The Consul removed the gavel from his ear and rapped with peremptory authority on the table.

'This court is held under the authority vested in me as Her Britannic Majesty's Consular Officer for the Coastal States. God Save the Queen!' A half-hearted murmur, as in some foreign tongue, ran round the court. The Consul attempted another sharp rap of the gavel but struck, instead of the table, the brim of his hat.

Flustered, he continued, 'This session is further to the meeting of . . .' he groped for the date in his papers and did not find it, 'er, last month. The verdict of the court at that time was to fine Duke Bosun', again he sought a figure and found none, 'a certain number of puncheons of palm-oil, only part of which has been yielded up.'

Duke Bosun was already on his feet, trampling his ju-ju man in his excitement. 'Fine be heavy too much. Trade done close for river too much. No be possible find all that oil one time.' He shuffled forward, hand extended beseechingly, face expressive of the many cares that weighed upon him. 'I be poor man now. No be rich like old time. I ask Consul he change fine. Too heavy for poor man like me. No be fit.'

The Consul made a shooing gesture and rapped his gavel. 'The fine was not fixed lightly and must stand.' Duke Bosun sat grouchily and continued to converse loudly with the empty air in Akwan. The Consul looked confused.

'Er, we are here to discuss another matter, the funeral festivities for Duke Bosun's sister, the Lady Iyalla. This matter has been raised by two concerned parties.' He looked down at his papers, 'Mr Nash and Reverend Truscot. Perhaps Mr Nash would be so kind as to speak his piece first.'

Both Nash and Truscot looked outraged at finding themselves sudden allies, butts of some dirty trick of coincidence.

Nash shambled to his feet, prefacing his remarks with a leonine snarl. 'I speak here for the traders of Akwa. I cannot speak for the missionaries – nor would I wish to. This has been a bad year for us. If Britain is to have the raw materials she needs to keep her industry going, it is only through the efforts of fellows like us, isolated here thousands of miles from our loved ones and the comforts of home, from all we hold dear . . .'

'Mr Nash. We are all in the same boat here,' the Consul looked around, 'quite literally.' He grinned at his own wit. 'There is no need to impress the court with the value of your activities to the Empire.'

Nash looked decidedly miffed to be interrupted. 'Quite.

Well. As I was saying. This war palaver has been ruinous for the trader. Trade has been shut off for months and is still not back to where it was. Some of our members have been foully slain – well, anyway Hauptmann was, at least we think he was.

'Overheads get heavier all the time, bleeding the white trader white. That is . . . well. You see what I mean. Over the past three years, freight costs have risen 10 per cent while the price of oil has dropped by 8. It gets harder and harder to make a living. We are faced with the prospect of chaps being recalled, their factories closed. You soon won't be able to get four white men together for a hand of cards. The foreigners won't be slow to move in to make a quick profit.

'Anyway, point is, we can't afford more trouble between Duketown and Akwa – not, of course, that we consider Duketown not to be part of Akwa, that is . . .

'This fighting has to stop. King Jack must disarm the bloodmen. Duties must be lowered to give relief to the trader. We can't have interference. It's up to the Consul to protect us. I think I can claim to be as God-fearing a man as any, but we can't have those who know nothing about it monkeying about with trade in the name of religion. Leads to nothing but trouble. Seen it happen loads of times. Er, that's it really.'

The traders whooped and applauded. Nash sat down, looking carefully behind before finally settling his buttocks on the chair, as if suspecting a misguided practical joker might have removed it.

'Reverend Truscot?'

Truscot rose and leaned forward, both hands on his cane.

'I am sorry that Mr Nash has felt moved to voice, yet again, his hostility to the works of God. I had hoped he might let bygones be bygones since there is no reason why, in the present matter, we might not have a common interest.

'The question is whether the law of Akwa is to be kept in

Akwa, whether the conditions agreed in treaties with the Consul are to be kept or simply ignored. In the treaty signed at the accession of King Jack, approved by your predecessor and with the mark of both King Jack and Duke Bosun, is a clause agreeing to abandon human sacrifice and permitting the Consul to intervene to punish any offenders. I offer a copy, kindly lent by King Jack, for the Consul's perusal.' He placed one deferentially on the table. 'On this matter, I think there can be no debate.

'Recently, contrary to the laws of God and the provisions of the treaty, Duke Bosun has resumed this practice. I have witnesses', he nodded to two shifty individuals at the back, 'who will testify that a considerable number of slaves were slain at Duke Bosun's plantation as part of the rites of interment of his sister, Iyalla.

'Like the bloodmen, who have hitherto posed no risk to public order and firm government, I ask simply that the great men of Akwa keep the laws of Akwa and show respect for the Consul. I therefore ask for the ultimate penalty against Duke Bosun.'

Scuttlebutt looked up from the treaty. 'What? What's that? Ultimate penalty? What do you mean? Exile? Heavy fine?'

'I ask', said Truscot with deliberation, 'for the ultimate penalty. To impose a fine is not enough to set the rule of law on Akwa. I ask for the head of' (he nearly said 'John the Baptist') 'Duke Bosun.'

A cry of disbelief ran round the court. Nash stood and began shouting about God-man interference and the primacy of trade. The Consul banged away with his gavel and shouted for order. King Jack smiled slightly.

As soon as the hubbub had subsided, Truscot spoke again. 'I am surprised', he raised an eyebrow to show that surprise, 'that the traders should be so hostile to a case that involves their own safety.' (Cries of 'Eh? What?') 'I have witnesses who will state that Mr Hauptmann was also killed as part of the festivities for

Iyalla, a white man killed in barbarous, shameful rites in a port where flies the Union Jack and the mail boat calls monthly.'

Duke Bosun rushed to the Consul's table and began to wrestle with it as though with an opponent. The Consul gripped it and sought to hold it down. The Hausas, rigid to attention, flicked an apprehensive smile at each other. The line allowing them to move would be crossed only if Duke Bosun picked up the table and hit the Consul with it.

'That no be so. I no chop Hauptmann. He bring me guns from Frenchman. For what I chop him?'

There was a silence. 'Aaah,' said Scuttlebutt. 'Did he now?' The traders went into a furious conclave. The witnesses concentrated hard on adapting the stories taught them by John Bull to these new circumstances. ('We see Hauptmann's guns before Bosun chop him or after? Maybe Bosun shoot him with those guns. No, he cut off head for him.') Truscot looked grim and red-faced. King Jack patted John Bull's head affectionately, tapping out his own drum name on the woolly pate.

Scuttlebutt banged his fist on the table, the gavel seeming suddenly inadequate to his strength of purpose.

'I find there is a *prima facie* case to answer against Duke Bosun for infringement of Clause Two of the Treaty of Accession, for murder of a foreign national under the protection of Her Majesty's Consul and for failure to pay a fine imposed by said Consul. I order him to be brought to trial and if found guilty, to suffer death. Penalty to be carried out by local custom. Palaver set!' He banged again.

Truscot sat down, completely drained. At home he would have to face Mary. She had wished to accompany him today, but her only suitable dress had been the brown one – now no longer in her possession.

The word 'justice' has little in it to mitigate the horror of taking human life. Yet I do honestly believe that if law is to be instituted where previously was only savagery, if the innocent are to be spared, then Duke Bosun must die. Only then will the air be purged so that we can make a new start in Akwa.

The bloodmen have returned to the plantations and I have praised their forbearance and discipline. They are good, simple people untainted by the vanity and corruption of the town. Many come to hear me speak when I visit them. They know now that the Church is the friend of the weak and dispossessed.

Poor Mary is rather poorly. In this climate the smallest wound becomes infected. Pricking her finger in a sewing class was enough to inspire a septic inflammation of the whole hand and sympathetic fever so that she needs must retire to her bed. Being at a low ebb spiritually, we felt the call to celebrate Communion to bring us back into fellowship with the Redeemer and slough off the shackles of this earthly life. The mission ship being overdue, we were in short supply of necessities and drank Our Saviour's blood in the form of Cuthbertson's Tonic Quinine Wine, a simultaneous remedy for the body and spirit. The taste was bitter yet sweet the blessing received. Text for a sermon here, I think. So many sermons as yet undelivered.

Duke Bosun's trial was a mere formality. The witnesses, schooled by John Bull, were well over their first-night nerves and lied with fluent conviction and elaborate circumstantial evidence. In an oral culture events rapidly become mythical. After a week – two at the most – there is no truth, just things that everyone knows. The traders were content that the slaying of a white man should be seen to be vigorously punished. Whether the accused was actually guilty or not was, to them, irrelevant. The Consul presided over the court with the professional bias of a committed patriot towards a confessed traitor. Duke Bosun turned the court against him by tediously refusing to admit himself guilty on all counts and then weeping in a most unmanly fashion as he railed against injustice. The actual verdict was reached by a committee composed of white traders and local chiefs. The death sentence found speedy approval from the Consul's hand, who added only that it was unfortunate the provisions of the treaty did not allow him to carry it out himself. His power was limited to seizing an amount of palm-oil from the man's goods, sufficient to pay the fine for previous ill conduct. This he did. Duke Bosun was led away to incarceration in Akwa, awaiting execution. A date was already set.

Truscot spent the morning of the execution alone in his study, reading in the Bible, seeking suitable precedent that would still his agony of mind. Mary came up behind him and lay a bandaged hand on his shoulder.

'You must not take this hard, Mannie. After all, it is the law.'

'Man's law, my dear, not necessarily God's. I still wonder whether those witnesses supplied by John Bull were really entirely honest. Yet, "an eye for an eye", "if thy hand offend thee, cut it" . . .' Oh, my dear, how stupid of me . . .' He looked guiltily at her swollen and visibly offending hand.

She laughed. 'It hasn't come to that yet.' She stared at him fondly. There was a sudden bang and the windows rattled. They both jumped.

'There it is then. The cannon in King Jack's yard. The execution is over.' Truscot sighed and lay the book aside. 'We must,' he said, 'think of life.' He looked at her and for once was purged of his normal shyness. 'My dear, I have never told you how proud I was of you during the plague, the way you looked after those poor women though far from well yourself. I never knew you had such strength and dedication.'

Mary blushed, unaccustomed to such bold words of praise. 'It was the Lord's work, Mannie. It had to be done.' She felt a surge of affection and took his hand comfortingly in her own bandaged grasp.

'Yes,' he said, as if relieved of a nagging illogicality, 'that would explain it then.' He dropped her hand and transferred his attention with a deliberate act of will to the birds swooping around the tree outside in the yard, only vaguely aware of Mary slamming the door as she left.

The rest of the day was spent playing with the twin children, numbers swollen by fresh arrivals, as if a Nature ignorant of Akwa culture were spontaneously trying to make good recent losses. By evening Truscot was pleasantly tired and purged of melancholy. Ali appeared at his elbow with a small glass of dark-red liquid. 'Quinine wine, *tuan*. This is the last.'

He should have thought of it before. 'Ali, take some of the cowries and manillas and use the boat to go to Mr Crosby's store. See if he can let you have a bottle – and some matches and candles, and anything else you think we are in need of.' Ali nodded and went back to the kitchen, knotting his sarong.

He hoped Crosby would not be childish about this. Well, there were other traders. If the worst came to the worst, he and Mary would live on yams and bananas till the ship turned up rather than be hostages to Crosby. He pottered across to his garden.

The maize was nearly ripe though it had suffered from birds and insects. Never mind. He did not begrudge them their tithe. There were melons sprouting pubescently. Beneath the mounds yams would be swelling to balance the sexual symmetry. He was content. He and Mary would dine lavishly on the fruits of his labours like dear old Adam and Eve.

Crosby's store was similar to many other such establishments on the Coast. It was a large shed really, shipped in sections from Liverpool and bolted together on the spot by Sierra Leone carpenters. Out here it would last about ten years before termites, the harsh alternation of the seasons and the intensive wear and tear of African usage reduced it to ruins. Then a new one would be erected a few yards further along the beach. Although only a few years old, this one was beset with unusual problems in that the blue hairy crabs had chosen to nest under one corner. Their constant excavations had undermined it to such a degree that it listed heavily to one side and the door could now be closed only by a bout of vigorous kicking. Crosby had done nothing to remedy this situation, largely because he found the kicking deeply therapeutic and expressive of his whole attitude to the Coast.

Shutters and door could be banged shut to maintain a sepulchral gloom, welcome relief from the glaring light outside. The tin roof radiated fierce heat, as in a Dutch oven, but the cement floor was permanently cool and pleasant to the touch. A broad mahogany counter ran the length of the store, defining the area for customers and dividing it off from the workspace of his spare and sallow clerks. Crosby treasured this barrier, the final and most solid of the many he had erected against Africa. Once behind it, he felt himself safe and fortified – in control. Ranged on shelves at his back, like loyal troops under his command, were the imported goods that were his stock in trade – brassware from Birmingham, cheap printed cloths from Manchester, knives and scissors from Sheffield, the whole industrial cornucopia of the world's greatest trading nation. From these he made the small but numerous individual sales to anyone who did not trade through the African middlemen. Behind the shelves lay the store-room, where he kept six months' supply of powder and shot. It satisfied him deeply to throw a flattened bale of cloth on to the polished mahogany top, flap out a few revolutions of the stuff so that its vibrant colours blazed in the gloom and haggle bitterly over the price with some African. Each successful sale was a defeat inflicted on this place, its climate and its people. Each time he pulled the cloth back, no sale made, he had refused to compromise, stood firm, defended the Empire.

Truscot's servant, that damned Chinese, stood the other side of his counter, ignoring the clerks as if he were white and expecting Crosby to serve him himself.

'What do you want here, boy?' A bubble of spittle formed and burst at the side of his mouth.

'Reverend Truscot sent me to ask for quinine wine, also certain other necessities.' He gently pushed a list across the counter.

'Certain other necessities.' Crosby see-sawed his head back and forth in mockery. 'Well, now.' He looked around at the well-stocked shelves. 'Oh, sorry! We seem to be out of just about all "necessities".'

Ali did not react, except that his face set into a deliberately blank expression.

'Please, *tuan*,' he spoke very quietly, 'I think you are mistaken. I think you look again. Look at the list.' The s's hissed like hot steel quenched in water. Crosby looked into the calm, dark irises and saw a world where men were warriors or were nothing, a world where honour and shame were more powerful than fear or profit. Cold sweat broke out along the creases of his forehead. He dithered and took the list. 'Wait. I'll look.' He stepped into the store-room and felt suddenly cold. He shook his head to clear it. Quinine wine? Well, he had some, but why not have a little fun? A smirk spread over his jowly face. He took a bottle to the barrel of red wine he sold to local chiefs and filled it. Quinine? He spooned in Epsom salts generously, put his thumb over the top and shook vigorously till the bottle emitted a wet fart of foam. That should do the Reverend nicely. He banged in a cork and gathered up the other goods, singing to himself.

'Here are your "necessities".' He saw the eyes again and

faltered. 'No, don't worry about paying. We don't need any more pictures of apostles. The Reverend's credit is good.' Ali nodded silently and padded out of the store on bare feet. Crosby got out his hip-flask and took a good tug.

The 'smokes' give way to the rains. The empty creeks are filling up. The river flows higher but in no way abates the attentions of the mosquitoes, who are as one of the plagues of Egypt. The waters are awash with river cabbages and the Akwa complain of poor fishing, claiming their quarry have returned to the spirit world to lobby for their interests at the annual convocation of the gods.

With the flow of the river, the internal tides of the human frame ebb and flood also. Mary and I find ourselves much afflicted by the flux, doubtless owing to the change of seasons and the reliance on the fresh and healthful produce from my garden. In remedy we abandon our teetotal preferences and take an extra tot of quinine wine. The greatest duty of the missionary is to be fit to work and theological dogma cannot be allowed to stand in the path of that necessity.

More news of my errant pupil, Adu. Tiring of her old husband, she entered into illicit relations with a young slave and ran away. Akwa law sees the offence as lying not in the adultery but the fact that a noblewoman has entertained a slave of her husband's house, which seems to be viewed as a sort of incest of mother with son. John Bull is furious against her and says that, if caught, she will suffer the terrible punishment whereby eyes, nose, mouth and *antrum mulieris* will be stuffed with chili. Some die of this handling. I see the fault as lying with this dreadful custom of polygamy, whereby a small number of old men monopolize the most sought-after young women, an offence against the heat of young blood and human decency. I spoke of it to my class. Many were dismayed to find that Christianity forbade them to have as many wives as the patriarchs. I explained the clarity of God's purpose that, as in the Garden of Eden, one man should cleave unto one woman, else half the world must go without a wife or know only adultery – unless slavery prevent it. Thus the entire order of ordained society, respect for law and human morality would be destroyed. Some seemed confused and argued that they themselves were slaves yet had several wives and wished to have more. What should they do, they asked, turn out their wives and children to starve? I see that passion undermines their reason in such matters, fuddling their thought, and fear this will become a major difficulty for our Church in the Delta. After my frank speaking, several pupils despaired of further enlightenment and departed my class. But I fear not. The wise farmer plucks out weeds ere they grow firm-rooted. I would have argued longer but the pressing need to void my bowels required me to desist.

The message came at nightfall. The rain had eased off and was ticking wetly as it percolated through the leaves of the plants and found its way back to the soil. The small boy wore only a strip of raffia-cloth around his loins and was silent as Will had been in his early days. Snot trails hung unheeded from his nose as if two large snails had recently exited from his nostrils. Ali gave him food and could not resist wiping his nose. The note was tightly sealed in a bamboo tube and written with charcoal on the back of a gin label carefully peeled off the bottle.

The orthography was wild and the grammar deformed, but it told Truscot all he needed to know. Adu was alone and frightened and did not know where else to turn for help. He would have to fetch her, bring her to the mission and try to intercede with King Jack. The small boy was brought in, wide-eyed, a roasted yam clutched messily in one hand. Where was the settlement? Far, massa. How far? One day by canoe. Which way? The boy pointed with the yam into the raucous darkness. That way, up-river. Very well, they would set off at dawn.

Truscot was weak from dysentery, his backside a scalded, raw patch like those of the monkeys of the forest. The ghost of a fever lurked behind his eyes. He took an extra tot of quinine and fell, ragged and thirsty, into bed.

When he woke, the rain had already started again. The downpour pushed the smoke back into the kitchen, made the house smaller and claustrophobic, rattled against doors and windows. He felt chilled, put on extra socks and greased boots, dipped ship's biscuit into tea and swallowed it down. The headache was still there. More quinine wine, then a dash to the soakaway privy, walled round with matting and flushed with heavy rain, where his breakfast squirted out pointlessly down the hole. His suffering was an offering he made to God. He hunched down in the canoe, the little boy in the prow pointing the way with a phlegmy gargle of Akwa. Ali settled behind him with the supplies. Two boatmen picked delicately through the water with their pointed paddles. Rain formed channels on their clothing and began to flow down into the boat. The journey lasted all day on the iron-grey water, the boatmen dodging through small channels in the mangrove swamps for hours, to suddenly burst through on to a major river only to branch off again. The rocking, slight though it was, made him nauseous. The boatmen's silence oppressed him. When they broke into song, it raged sickeningly in his head. He ordered them into the bank repeatedly to relieve himself, returning shivering and weakened to the boat, fractiously swatting away the mosquitoes and then just ignoring them. Ghosts of previous voidings screwed and gurgled through his guts. By the evening, he was delirious. Ali ordered the boat to turn round.

Truscot came to in the mission. The journey had been just a dream then, a nightmare of the fever. His hands were dotted with bites. He looked at them wonderingly as they lay on the sheets. How had that happened?

Mary was sitting by the bed, her face wan and lined. At first she did not realize he had recovered consciousness and her lips moved thinly in prayer. Then she saw his eyes move and uttered a little cry.

'Adu?' he asked. 'What happened to Adu?'

She sobbed, 'Oh, Mannie! You never got there. The fever. She had gone anyway. King Jack has her now. Think of yourself. Think of me. What should I do here alone? There's no more you can do but rest.' The voice trailed off in a wail stifled by her handkerchief.

Ali entered, pleased to see Truscot recovered, offered broth and more quinine. 'Funny,' mumbled Truscot, 'can't taste quinine at all. You'd think it was just wine. Mary, Mary.'

She bent forward and whispered, 'Yes, Mannie?' A message of love? Instructions concerning what to do if . . .?

'Mary . . . Mother of God.' He snickered uncharacteristically. A vision of bookmarks sailed before his eyes. 'Damned Popery.'

Then the fever came upon him again. His last sight was of Mary sucking the corner of her handkerchief in terror and Ali with a slow tear that began from the corner of his eye. By the time it fell Truscot was dead.

They trudged miserably through the water, the pools rife with insolent life. The widow had returned to a stunned calm, her grief still boiling within her in a way that must surely soon erupt again.

'King Jack. I would ask you one last favour. It was my husband's dying wish. You know in our country such a thing is nearly sacred.' She was working away internally, redefining her life. Her husband was perfect and without fault. Already he had become a totem, the rest of her life a monument.

King Jack nodded wonderingly.

'It is Adu. I beg you. Be kind to her. Forgive her faults. Take her back to your family.' It was not quite true, but this was what Mannie's final words should perhaps have been. There was a regal detachment about widowhood that appealed to something deep inside her.

'I will, Missus. I be kind to her like her own fadder.' He grinned. No one else smiled.

'What is that?' They had come to the outer edge of the 'bad bush'. A sapling had been driven into the ground and painted with black and white stripes after the fashion of a barber's pole. On the top was a bundle. Curiosity momentarily drove out her sadness and widow's dignity.

'Duke Bosun palaver, Missus.' They coughed and shuffled their feet.

'Oh! Oh, I see. Duke Bosun's head.' It left her unmoved, merely mildly embarrassed. She must be cauterized by the grief of losing Mannie. He had suffered over that business, but she had never doubted that he had done the right thing. He had left Akwa more in harmony with God's laws than he had found it.

'No, Missus. No be Bosun himself.' With a courtly solicitude, the King pushed back the branch overshadowing the face, as one would hold open a door for a lady. 'Duke Bosun be gentleman. He no die. We no kill gentleman. No be fit for Akwa law. We kill slave in his place.' She stared into a face familiar despite the rictus of death and the onset of putrefaction. Here was not the luxuriant, unbroken brow of Duke Bosun but a countenance that combined surprise with a certain quiet reproach. 'You did not', it said, 'send the money' – the face of Silent Will.

'Best thing really,' said Nash, looking after the departing ship. 'Don't want people like that stirring up the natives, people who don't understand the country. No place for a white woman. If you *have* to have missionaries, get in some professionals, like that bunch down in Calabar. They seem to understand local ways. Don't monkey about with polygamy, none of this "black fella got soul all same white fella" tosh. Plenty of hell-fire and damnation – "you're all the damned sons of Ham" business.

That's the stuff to give 'em. Fear of God makes 'em jump about a bit.' The ship had reached the main river channel and was sniffing around like a dog, its snout to the open sea.

'Couldn't agree more,' said Jones. 'Still, it'll feel odd without them. So few whites about these days. Since Crosby and all.' They contemplated the thought in silence. Crosby had slit his own throat – pretty near cut his own head off as some said – in the crow's-nest of his hulk. It was an odd way to do it, but there was no doubt his death had come by his own hand – unless, that was, there was anyone who could shin up forty feet of smooth mast, do such a thing silently and exit without trace – for his servants had been laying the table at the base of the stairs when he died. Even under threat of saucy water they had maintained their story, so there was no doubting it. It was well known that natives could never agree to a false story and stick to it in the face of white interrogation. There had been short-comings in the accounts – the usual sort of thing, a history of fever, drink. It had all happened before. Nash had acted quickly to hush up the scandal. A bad business though.

Ali looked back from the ship at the headland. It seemed to him that a ray of sunshine was playing on the spot where he and John Bull had buried the Reverend. Ali had been determined that *tuan* should not lie in an unclean place, but the one he had spoken of that evening when he had been sad and talked of death. Ali knew that such moments must be respected. They came from God – like the time when you suddenly knew it was right for you to leave on the pilgrimage to Mecca. They had washed the body and wrapped it in white sheets – though John Bull had wanted to use the blue ju-ju curtains – weighting down the empty box with rocks rare as gold on these mud flats. It had taken hours to collect them, but they had not begrudged the effort. Over the mound Ali had planted a rose bush. They had not been able to give a Christian burial but that was unimportant. It was the place that was right. Anyway, just to be on the safe side, Ali had read the Koran – sections of which he knew were in the Christian book – over the grave. John Bull had joined in in parts. Already, he knew the prayers quite well.